SUPER GENIUS
ENVIRONMENT QUIZ

SUPER GENIUS
ENVIRONMENT QUIZ

Dilip M. Salwi

RUPA

Published by
Rupa Publications India Pvt. Ltd 2004
7/16, Ansari Road, Daryaganj
New Delhi 110002

Sales centres:
Allahabad Bengaluru Chennai
Hyderabad Jaipur Kathmandu
Kolkata Mumbai

ISBN: 978-81-716-7022-2

Fifth impression 2018

10 9 8 7 6 5

The moral right of the author has been asserted.

Typeset by Tarun Enterprises, Delhi

To
A friend and
well-wisher
Praveen Kadam for his
friendly and helpful nature

HELLO! ENVIRONMENT QUIZ BUFFS!

Nowadays, the subject of environment has become something like weather. Everybody talks about it but nobody does anything about it! I had written *'1000 Environment Quiz'* more than a decade ago with the hope that it would give everybody a flavour of what it is all about and remove certain misunderstandings about it. The very fact the book has gone into several reprints speaks volumes about people's interest in the subject. But I must add that the response to the book had not been as much as I had expected then. In those days, environment was a very hot subject and the media was full of it. But today it has taken a back seat as the country has gone in for liberalisation and privatisation, though the subject is being seriously taught in schools, colleges and universities. Even graduate and post-graduate courses in the subject have been offered by several colleges and universities. Let's hope the coming young generation would not simply talk about environment but would do something concrete to save all of us from the onslaught of technology. I have revised the aforementioned book, adding some new questions here and there, and also divided it into two parts with new titles to suit the Super Quiz series that I have started. I am sure, they would go a long way in inculcating interest in environment as a life-long passion and career. All the best, quiz buffs!

Dilip M. Salwi

Acknowledgements

I am specially thankful to Dr N.R. Mankad for going through the manuscript patiently and suggesting changes, etc., on various aspects of the book. I am also thankful to the following persons and organisations for supplying me with photographs published in the book: Asok Samanta, Manager, Photo Archives, American Center, New Delhi; Gopi Menon of the USSR Information Center, New Delhi; Malti Jaikumar and Ravi Datta of the British Information Service, New Delhi; the CEDUST, New Delhi; Inter Nationes, Germany; Meteorologie Nationale, France; Imperial Chemical Industries Limited, U.K.; Kapur Farms, New Delhi; and Sunita Narain, Director, Centre for Science and Environment, New Delhi. Last but not the least I am thankful to my wife Smriti, daughter Neha and son Romel for bearing with me while I was busy revising the book.

Dilip M. Salwi

CONTENTS

I

TRAIL BLAZERS

Pathfinders

1. Who showed that both American eels and European eels spawn at the bottom of the Sargasso sea?
   (a) Maurice B. Otis   (b) John Dory
   (c) E. Johannes Schmidt
   (d) John Ray

2. Who started scientific bird banding for studying migratory behaviour of birds?
   (a) Christian Mortensen
   (b) A.J. Berger
   (c) Salim Ali   (d) J.C.Welty

3. Who discovered a herd of a new type of deer in Peking's Imperial park and shipped some to European zoos, thus saving them from total extinction today?
   (a) Heinz Heck   (b) Peter Scott
   (c) Joy Adamson   (d) Pere Armand David

4. Which ice-related phenomenon was spotted by a satellite?

(a) Iceberg   (b) Polynya
(c) Glacier   (d) None

5. Who formulated this ecological principle: 'The presence and success of an organism or a group of organisms depends upon a complex of conditions. Any condition that approaches or exceeds the limits of tolerance is said to be a limiting condition or a limiting factor'?
   (a) E.P. Odum   (b) V.I. Vernadsky
   (c) Aldo Leopold   (d) Frank Fraser Darling

6. Who obtained about 300 different products from peanuts?
   (a) Charles H. Herty   (b) Austin W. Curtis
   (c) George Washington Carver
   (d) William J. Morse

7. Who gave the theory of 'Life zones'?
   (a) Leslie Holdridge   (b) Charles Elton
   (c) E. P. Odum   (d) C. Hart Merriam

8. Which satellite recorded the presence of an ozone hole?
   (a) *TIROS-N*   (b) *GOES*
   (c) *Nimbus-7*   (d) *Landsat-3*

9. Who discovered natural radioactivity?
   (a) Pierre Curie   (b) Marie Curie
   (c) Henri Becquerel   (d) All

10. Who formulated the ecological concept of the 'Pyramid of Numbers'?
    (a) Charles Elton   (b) Paul R. Ehrlich
    (c) Paul Colinvaux   (d) Lamont C . Cole

11. Who discovered the method of determining the age of a whale?
    (a) Roger Payne   (b) Andrew E. Douglas
    (c) J. T. Rudd   (d) Francis M. Balfour

12. Who dramatically demonstrated that an epidemic of typhoid and cholera in London was from a well that was polluted by nearby sewers?
    (a) Ronald Ross   (b) Emil Behring
    (c) John Snow   (d) Hans Gram

13. Which satellite spotted what are known as 'Van Allen radiation belts'?
    (a) *Uburu*   (b) *Vanguard*
    (c) *Explorer-I*   (d) *IRAS*

Propounders

14. Which conservationist advocated the development of an ecological conscience?
    (a) Gerald Durrell   (b) Madhav Gadgil
    (c) Eric Eckholm   (d) Aldo Leopold

15. Who believed that climatic observations were important to increase the progress of human knowledge?
    (a) John Dalton   (b) Gilbert Walker
    (c) Abraham Lincoln (d) Thomas Jefferson

16. Who forwarded the Gaia hypothesis, which claims that the earth is alive and functions as a super organism?
    (a) Richard Dawkins (b) James Lovelock
    (c) James Hutton   (d) Lewis Thomas

17. Who decreed futilely as far ago as in 1681 that one acre of forest must be left in an area for every five acres cleared?
    (a) John Ray   (b) William Penn
    (c) Rene Descartes   (d) Francesco Redi

18. Who preached reverence for all living things?
    (a) Mahatma Gandhi   (b) Martin Luther King
    (c) S. Radhakrishnan (d) Albert Schweitzer

19. Who forwarded the idea of a 'Planet Protection Fund' to protect the environment of the world at the U.N. General Assembly?
    (a) Shridath Ramphal (b) Malcolm Fraser
    (c) Javier Perez de Cuellar
    (d) Rajiv Gandhi

20. Which philosopher and writer saw the natural

environment as an outlet, an 'open end' to civilisation?

(a) Ralph Waldo Emerson
(b) Henry David Thoreau
(c) Alvin Toffler
(d) Jean Jacques Rousseau

21. Who believes that science is on the verge of discovering the metabolism of the earth?
    (a) Paul Hays   (b) Stephen Schneider
    (c) Carl Sagan   (d) James Lovelock

22. Which body claimed way back in 1972, that, 'if the present growth trends in world population, industrialisation, pollution, food production, and resource depletion continue unchanged, the limits to growth on this planet will be reached some time within the next 100 years'?
    (a) The United Nations
    (b) The Club of Rome
    (c) The Green Party   (d) Caltech

23. Who proposed the idea of Debt-for-Nature swap, which is fast catching up all over the world?
    (a) Deborah Burand   (b) Thomas E. Lovejoy
    (c) Maurice Strong   (d) None

24. Who is the founder of biogeochemistry?

(a) Richard Dawkins   (b) Paul R. Ehrlich
(c) V.I. Vernadsky   (d) Julian Huxley

Coining Things

25. Who coined the phrase 'Tyranny of small decisions' to describe the petty and short-sighted decisions which lead to ecological degradation and destruction?
    (a) Kenneth E. Boulding
    (b) Alfred E. Kahn
    (c) V. Tarzie Vittachi (d) Paul Harrison

26. Who called man an 'Ecologically dominant' organism?
    (a) Ruth Benedict   (b) Frank Boas
    (c) Carl Sauer   (d) Margaret Mead

27. Who called our era the ' Age of Poisons'?
    (a) Robert Heilbroner (b) Gerald Durrell
    (c) Rachel Carson   (d) Jawaharlal Nehru

28. Who coined the phrase 'Biological pump' for the means by which life in the ocean draws carbon dioxide from the air and dispatches it from top layers to the depths?
    (a) Roger Revelle
    (b) Michael McElory
    (c) Norman Cousins

(d) Nicholas Shackleton

29. Who coined the word 'Megalopolis'?
    (a) Lewis Mumford   (b) Patrick Geddes
    (c) Norman Cousins   (d) Jean Gottman

30. Who coined the term 'Eco-development'?
    (a) Barbara Ward   (b) Rene Dubos
    (c) W.W. Rostow   (d) Maurice Strong

31. Who coined the phrase 'Global village' for an electronically close-knit world?
    (a) Bertrand Russell (b) Marshall McLuhan
    (c) E.F. Schumacher   (d) Mahatma Gandhi

32. Who changed the name of Kubabul, one of the popular tree species suited for afforestation, to Subabul?
    (a) Manibhai Desai   (b) Lal Bahadur Shastri
    (c) A.K.N. Reddy   (d) Indira Gandhi

33. Who reiterated the phrase of the English poet John Donne 'No man is an island' in his ecological writings?
    (a) U Thant   (b) Thomas Merton
    (c) Barry Commoner   (d) Arnold Toynbee

34. Who coined 'Ekistics' – the science of human settlements?
    (a) Margaret Mead   (b) C.A. Doxiadis
    (c) Both   (d) None

35. Who coined the slogan 'Act locally, think globally'?
    (a) Peter Kropotkin   (b) Petra Kelly
    (c) William Gilpin   (d) Anonymous

Crusaders

36. Which conservationist believed that it is our duty as members of the human race to pass on to posterity a natural world that is still worth living in?
    (a) Salim Ali   (b) S. Dillon Ripley
    (c) Norman Myers   (d) Peter Scott

37. Who is the founder of Birdland, the bird sanctuary in the Cotswolds, U.K.?
    (a) Peter Scott   (b) Richard Hill
    (c) Lee Durrell   (d) Gerald Durrell

38. Who died in 1988 fighting for the rainforest of the Amazon basin?
    (a) Jorge Gomes Pinheiro
    (b) Wilson Pinheiro
    (c) Nigel Lawson
    (d) Francisco Mendes Filho

39. Which animal's Latin name is after E.P. Gee, a famous conservationist, who brought it into limelight?

(a) Brown Bear
(b) Golden Langur
(c) Fishing Cat
(d) Gaur

40. Who is often referred to as the 'Man of the Trees'?
(a) Sundarlal Bahuguna
(b) Baba Amte
(c) Chand Prasad Bhatt
(d) Richard St. Barbe Baker

41. Who established the Talavaya Center in New Mexico to preserve ancient seed strains of the local community?
(a) Bob Geldof
(b) John Kimmey
(c) John Horsman
(d) All

42. Who has founded the Owl Rehabilitation Research Foundation in Canada to treat injured owls, breed them, and release them into the wild?
(a) Larry and Kay McKeever
(b) Sue and Les Stocker
(c) Sue Russell   (d) Shirley McGreal

43. Who has been fighting for more than 40 years to save the last big stretch of tropical

rainforest in central America?
(a) Alison Richard   (b) Robert Betz
(c) Hernan Cortes   (d) Gertrude Blom

44. Who has built several shelters and hospitals in Delhi for animals and birds?
(a) Usha Ganguli   (b) Crystal Rogers
(c) Iqbal Malik   (d) Diana Ratnagar

45. Who believed that the only way to attack the problem of deforestation 'is to recreate a system within the society, which will then feel that growing and supporting trees is crucial to its own survival'?
(a) Bo Landin   (b) Anil Aggarwal
(c) Salim Ali   (d) Viktor Sebek

II

LIFE ON EARTH

Life and Habitat

46. Where are Musk Oxen found?
    (a) Greenland   (b) New Zealand
    (c) Antarctica   (d) Norway

47. Which of the following mammals can survive without water for a whole year?
    (a) Wild Ass   (b) Gembok
    (c) Addax   (d) None

48. Which animal's habits and habitat are as yet unknown?
    (a) Himalayan Palm Civet
    (b) Red Fox
    (c) Palla's Cat
    (d) Himalayan Squirrel

49. Which of the following animals lives at the greatest height?
    (a) Urial   (b) Nilgiri Tahr
    (c) Wild Yak   (d) Goral

50. Which is the place where no mammal originally lived?

(a) Myanmar (b) Japan
(c) Thailand (d) New Zealand

51. Where are the fastest runners in the world found?
    (a) Tropical forests (b) Grassland
    (c) Tundras (d) Deserts

52. Where are the world's freshwater seals found?
    (a) Baikal Lake (b) Loch Broom
    (c) Lake of the Woods
    (d) Lake Tanganyika

53. Which of the following marine beings uses echo-location to sense its prey and surrounding environment?
    (a) Baleen Whale (b) Weddell Seal
    (c) Walrus (d) All

54. Which of the following mammals is an inhabitant of coastal waters, estuaries, and slow-moving rivers?
    (a) Hippopotamus (b) Walrus
    (c) Whale (d) Manatee

55. Which is the only species of seals that inhabits the Mediterranean sea?
    (a) Monk Seal (b) Leopard Seal
    (c) Bearded Seal (d) Grey Seal

56. Which of the following fishes is the inhabitant

of scattered water bodies in a desert?
(a) Rainbow Wrasse
(b) Viviparous Blenny
(c) Five-breaded Rockling
(d) Devil's Hole Pupfish

57. Which fish lives in freshwater, breeds in Sargasso sea and returns?
(a) Garfish
(b) Eel
(c) Mackerel
(d) Shad

58. Which fish does a double-loop migration in the warmer regions of the Pacific?
(a) Opah
(b) Hake
(c) Grunion
(d) Albacore

59. Which is the only place in Europe where flamingos nest?
(a) Coto Donana, Spain
(b) Bialowieza National Park, Poland
(c) Minsmere Bird Reserve, UK
(d) Camargue, France

60. Which island is an exclusive bird reserve?
(a) Antigua Island
(b) Grenada Island
(c) Niue Island
(d) Cousin Island

61. Which bird lives throughout its life in tundra regions?
(a) Arctic Tern
(b) Red Phalarope

(c) Rock Ptarmigan

(d) Bristle-thighed Curlew

62. Which is the only bird known to live in caves?
    (a) Guacharo   (b) Hoatzin
    (c) Guillemot   (d) Puffin

63. Which is the powerfully built sea-bird that makes nests in either the Arctic or Antarctic region?
    (a) Shearwater   (b) Adelie Penguin
    (c) Skua   (d) Pelican

64. Which group of plants is sensitive to airborne chemicals and are therefore used as pollution indicators?
    (a) Algae   (b) Lichens
    (c) Fungi   (d) Bryophytes

65. Which tree is popular as 'Green Gold' yet it is an ecological disaster?
    (a) Grey Alder   (b) Eucalyptus
    (c) Apricot   (d) Coconut Palm

66. Which are the most successful and widespread of all land plants?
    (a) Weeds   (b) Fungi
    (c) Lichens   (d) Grasses

67. Which plant stabilises the sand and prevents its erosion by wind?

(a) Eel Grass   (b) Beach Grass
(c) Sea Sandwort   (d) Prickly Saltwort

68. Which insect entered the USA and infested the whole of the cotton belt at the turn of the present century?
    (a) Wooly Aphid
    (b) Black Bean Aphid
    (c) Boll Weevil
    (d) Pea Weevil

69. Which of the following organisms can survive a temperature as high as 92°C?
    (a) Desert Lizards   (b) Algae
    (c) Camels   (d) Vultures

70. Which creature's activity improves soil texture, surface infiltration and drainage?
    (a) Dung Beetle   (b) Cockohafer
    (c) Earthworm   (d) Violet Ground Beetle

71. Which of the following marine beings migrates vertically daily?
    (a) Amphipods   (b) Decapods
    (c) Copepods   (d) Mysids

72. Where is the world's largest species of endangered butterflies — Queen Alexandra's birdwing — found?

(a) Madagascar   (b) Papua New Guinea
(c) Philippines   (d) Venezuela

Wildlife

73. A tiger will think twice before attacking this animal, even though it is alone. Which is it?
    (a) Nilgai   (b) Wild Dog
    (c) Wild Buffalo   (d) Chital

74. Which of the following animals makes a whistling sound to communicate with others of its kind when it senses danger or prey?
    (a) Indian Fox   (b) Red Fox
    (c) Striped Hyena   (d) Indian Wild Dog

75. Which monkey is active during the night and rests during the day?
    (a) Lion-tailed Macaque
    (b) Nilgiri Langur
    (c) South American Douroucouli
    (d) Bonnet Macaque

76. Which is the terrestrial mammal that uses infrasound — sound below the range of human hearing — for communication?
    (a) Monkey   (b) Lion
    (c) Elephant   (d) None

77. Which of the following big animals is migratory?
    (a) Elk   (b) Reindeer
    (c) Caribou   (d) Wild Boar

78. Which of the following animals conserves moisture by reusing its body water?
    (a) Hill Kangaroo (b) Kangaroo Rat
    (c) Devil Lizard   (d) Puff Adder

79. Where in the world is located the only known population of Black-footed Ferrets?
    (a) Wyoming, USA   (b) Carolina, USA
    (c) Peru   (d) Argentina

80. What does a Koala Bear eat?
    (a) Bamboo shoots (b) Walnut
    (c) Eucalyptus leaves (d) Barberry

81. Which animals digs out a den in snow for living and cub-rearing?
    (a) Weddell Seal   (b) Snow Leopard
    (c) Leopard Seal   (d) Polar Bear

82. Which species of monkeys is the hardiest?
    (a) Chimpanzee   (b) Gibbon
    (c) Macaque   (d) Langur

Domesticated Life

83. Which country has the largest population of cattle?
    - (a) China
    - (b) India
    - (c) Russia
    - (d) Australia

84. Which of the following pet animals practices internal fertility control?
    - (a) Dog
    - (b) Turtle
    - (c) Cat
    - (d) Rabbit

85. Elephants of one region cannot be domesticated. Which region?
    - (a) Myanmar
    - (b) Borneo
    - (c) Sumatra
    - (d) Kenya

86. Where is listening to recorded bird-songs a pastime?
    - (a) USA
    - (b) Canada
    - (c) Russia
    - (d) Australia

87. Which of the following type of sheep is a rare species?
    - (a) Great Tibetan Sheep
    - (b) Marco Polo's Sheep
    - (c) Blue Sheep
    - (d) None

88. Which of the following animals is domesticated?

(a) Gaur (b) Banteng
(c) Yak
(d) Wild Buffalo

89. To which group do domesticated animals which human beings eat belong to?
(a) Carnivores (b) Herbivores
(c) Omnivores (d) Predators

90. Which fish has been domesticated on a large scale by man in the recent past?
(a) Mackerel (b) Sturgeon
(c) Tilapia (d) Mullet

91. Which type of monkey is tamed to perform street-shows?
(a) Assamese Macaque
(b) Hanuman Langur
(c) Lion-tailed Macaque
(d) Bonnet Macaque

92. Which city was the main route of export of parrots to the West some time ago?
(a) London
(b) Amsterdam
(c) Manila
(d) Madrid

Endangered Life

93. Where was the Tasmanian Tiger, the world's rarest animal today, once found in abundance?
    (a) Australia (b) New Zealand
    (c) Hawaii (d) China

94. Which of the following birds is on the verge of extinction from loss of habitat?
    (a) Great Tit (b) Bald Ibis
    (c) Black-billed Magpie
    (d) Pied Avocet

95. Which of the following animals is on the verge of extinction from hunting?
    (a) Moose deer (b) Dik-dik
    (c) Spanish Ibex (d) Thomson Gazelle

96. Which creature has become rare as a result of loss of habitat?
    (a) Cricket Frog (b) Cuban Tree Frog
    (c) Majorcan Midwife Toad
    (d) Gulf Coast Toad

97. Which of the following plants has become rare as a result of loss of habitat?
    (a) Meadow Rues (b) Monkey Flower
    (c) Maltese Fungus (d) Asparagus Fern

98. Which of the following animals is on the verge

of extinction from loss of habitat and extensive hunting?

(a Pine Marten   (b) African Linsang

(c) Maned Wolf   (d) Spanish Lynx

99. Which of the following animals was once believed to be extinct but has now been found to be flourishing?

(a) Leopard Cat   (b) Striped Hyena

(c) Indian Fox   (d) Pigmy Hog

100. Which of the following fish is an endangered species?

(a) Sprat   (b) Anglerfish

(c) Snail Darter   (d) Greenland Halibut

101. Which of the following species of primates is on the endangered list?

(a) Siamang

(b) Hanuman Langur

(c) Cottontop Tamarin

(d) Squirrel Monkey

102. Which plant, though the best-known of all house plants, is the most endangered one in the wild?

(a) African Violet   (b) Common Ivy

(c) Mistletoe Fig   (d) Pink Jasmine

Extinct Life

103. What caused the extinction of the bird Dodo?
    (a) Beautiful feathers
    (b) Fearlessness
    (c) Curved beak   (d) Melodious songs

104. Which of the following birds became extinct in recent times?
    (a) Kirtland's Warbler
    (b) Carolina Parakeet
    (c) Atitlan Grebe
    (d) Reed Bunting

105. Which of the following animals was once abundant in India but is now extinct?
    (a) Asiatic Cheetah
    (b) Hoolock Gibbon
    (c) Lion-tailed Macaque
    (d) Himalayan Tahr

106. Where were the now-extinct Moas, the huge grazing birds, found?
    (a) Brazil   (b) Argentina
    (c) Kenya   (d) New Zealand

107. Which of the following animals is extinct today?
    (a) Quagga
    (b) Przewalski Horse

(c) Pere David's Deer

(d) Giant Panda

108. Which food plant once commonly found in Somalia and Ethiopia is today on the brink of exinction from war, famine and goats?

(a) Hottentot Fig (b) Jojoba

(c) Yeheb   (d) All

109. Which of the following Indian birds is extinct today?

(a) Blacknecked Crane

(b) Blewitt's Spotted Owlet

(c) Grey Pelican

(d) Malabar Pied Hornbill

110. Which bird once migrated across the USA in huge flocks but was exterminated in large numbers and as a result is today an extinct species?

(a) Gull-billed Tern

(b) Red Knot

(c) Mallard

(d) Passenger Pigeon

111. Which of the following sea-bird is extinct today?

(a) Guillemot   (b) Razorbill

(c) Puffin   (d) Great Auk

III

INTERFERENCE WITH NATURE

Human Settlements

112. Which material has been used in all building activities since pre-historic times?
    (a) Pegmatite   (b) Limestone
    (c) Granite   (d) Laterite

113. Where has the oldest road in the world been found?
    (a) Iraq   (b) Egypt
    (c) England   (d) Peru

114. What has forced man to destroy forests?
    (a) Cultivate food (b) Build cities
    (c) Graze his domesticated animals
    (d) All

115. In which age did man first cultivate crops and domesticate animals?
    (a) Palaeolithic Age
    (b) Bronze Age
    (c) Iron Age
    (d) Neolithic Age

116. What were sheep initially domesticated for?
    (a) Meat   (b) Milk
    (c) Fur   (d) Oil

117. Where has the oldest human structure, a hunting shelter, been found?
    (a) Nice, France
    (b) Mohenjo-daro, Pakistan
    (c) Lothal, India
    (d) Belmonte, Brazil

118. When did men live by spear, bow and fishing net?
    (a) Iron Age   (b) Mesolithic Age
    (c) Neolithic Age (d) Bronze Age

119. Where has the earliest big town in the world been found?
    (a) Italy   (b) India
    (c) Pakistan   (d) Turkey

120. Where is Asia's largest slum located?
    (a) Kolkata   (b) Mumbai
    (c) Delhi   (d) Chennai

121. Which city instituted the world's first planned and administered programme of forest conservation?
    (a) Venice   (b) Barcelona
    (c) Kolkata   (d) Tripoli

122. Where was the horse first tamed?
   (a) China   (b) Iran
   (c) Iraq   (d) Peru

123. Where were sewers invented?
   (a) India   (b) Assyria
   (c) Greece   (d) Italy

124. What is inadvertently causing a fast deterioration of the environment all over the world?
   (a) Fast evolution of technologies
   (b) Slow evolution of technologies
   (c) Evolution of crude technologies
   (d) Evolution of eco-friendly technologies

125. What is an e-waste?
   (a) Silicon chip
   (b) Cathode Ray Tube
   (c) Printed Circuit Board
   (d) All

126. What does e-waste mainly consist of?
   (a) Lead   (b) Mercury
   (c) Beryllium   (d) All

127. Which type of family is the most eco-friendly?
   (a) Joint family
   (b) Nuclear family

(c) Single parent family
(d) Single living

Population

128. Who gave the slogan, 'Development is the best contraceptive'?
    (a) Karan Singh
    (b) M.K. Tolba
    (c) David Dickson
    (d) E.F. Schumacher

129. Which country launched a campaign urging parents to have only one child to control population pressure?
    (a) China   (b) India
    (c) South Korea (d) Kenya

130. What does the most widely used chemical contraceptive contains?
    (a) Oestrogen   (b) Prolactin
    (c) Testosterone (d) Progestogen

131. Who remarked, '...nothing is more likely to lead to an H-bomb war than the threat of universal destitution through overpopulation'?
    (a) George Bernard Shaw
    (b) Bertrand Russell

(c) Robert Malthus

(d) Lester R. Brown

132. Which century is known as the 'Century of Refugees'?
    (a) 16th   (b) 17th
    (c) 19th   (d) 20th

133. Who wrote 'The Population Bomb' predicting that a quarter of mankind would starve to death between
    1973 and 1983?
    (a) Paul R. Ehrlich (b) Frank Barnaby
    (c) Margaret Mead (d) Erik Eckholm

134. Which is the first country in the world to adopt a national family planning programme?
    (a) Nigeria   (b) Kenya
    (c) India   (d) Iran

135. What is the population growth curve of a living being in a new habitat?
    (a) Sigmoid-shaped form
    (b) 8-shaped form
    (c) U-shaped form
    (d) Bell-shaped form

136. Who said, 'The human population explosion is in fact the worst and basic form of pollution'?

28

 (a) E.F. Schumander
 (b) K. Curry Lindahl
 (c) Susan George
 (d) Charles Medawar

137. Every dam's construction leads to displacement of a large population of people. Which dam's construction led to the highest displacement of population?
 (a) Kariba dam (b) Bhakra dam
 (c) Aswan High dam
 (d) Ubolratana dam

138. Nearly one-third of the human population lives within 65 kilometres of this. What is it?
 (a) a river (b) a forest
 (c) a glacier (d) a sea

Man-made Migrations: Plants

139. Which is the native place of Soyabean?
 (a) Egypt (b) Japan
 (c) China (d) Indonesia

140. Which was the first New World plant to take root in tne soil of the Old World?
 (a) Cotton (b) Potato
 (c) Peanut (d) Tomato

141. Which is the native place of Watermelon?

(a) Africa
(b) South America
(c) North America
(d) Australia

142. Which shrub brought from Australia to decorate garden hedges in India has become a weed?
    (a) Rock rose   (b) Lantana
    (c) Bilberry   (d) Elder

143. Which is the native place of Tea?
    (a) Indonesia   (b) India
    (c) Thailand   (d) China

144. Christopher Columbus brought some native grains from Cuba to Europe, where they were cultivated and then distributed to the entire world. What were those grains?
    (a) Barley   (b) Wheat
    (c) Maize   (d) Rice

145. From where was Eucalyptus brought to Europe?
    (a) Australia   (b) Africa
    (c) South America (d) North America

146. Which is the native place of Cocoa?
    (a) Greenland   (b) New Zealand
    (c) South America (d) Antarctica

147. From where was Tobacco brought to Europe?
    (a) South America (b) Africa
    (c) Australia   (d) North America

148. Which is the native place of Bananas?
    (a) Arabia   (b) India
    (c) Tibet
    (d) North America

Man-made Migration: Living Beings

149. Which of the following animals originated in North America, crossed over to Asia, and became extinct in its place of origin until re-introduced by man?
    (a) Cat   (b) Dog
    (c) Horse   (d) Bison

150. Which 'foreign' fish introduced accidentally into the American Great Lakes depleted their population of game fish?
    (a) Gudgeon   (b) Roach
    (c) Lamprey   (d) Sturgeon

151. Which animal, when introduced into New Zealand, led to severe soil erosion in the countryside?
    (a) Cat   (b) Goat
    (c) Horse   (d) Deer

152. Which insect was imported from Australia

into the USA to bring another insect under control which had destroyed citrus orchards?
(a) Ladybird *Adalia bipunctato*
(b) Beetle *Oxyporus rufus*
(c) Beetle *Emus hirtus*
(d) Ladybird *Novius cardinalis*

153. Which animal, when introduced into Australia, upset the ecological balance of the countryside?
(a) Cat   (b) Monkey
(c) Rabbit   (d) Jerbil

154. Which of the following birds was imported from Europe to North America to give the latter a touch of the former?
(a) House Sparrow
(b) Parrot
(c) Passenger Pigeon
(d) Crow

155. Who brought the horse to North America?
(a) French explorers
(b) Spanish explorers
(c) English explorers
(d) Early English settlers

156. Which big animal was imported into New Zealand?
(a) Scottish Red Deer

(b) Elk
(c) Reindeer
(d) Black Buck

157. Which fish was introduced into several tropical regions to control malaria?
 (a) Halibut
 (b) Minnow
 (c) Gambusia
 (d) Carp

158. Which is basically the native place of the European Rabbit?
 (a) England
 (b) The Mediterranean region
 (c) India
 (d) China

159. Which living being accidently reached a German port in the ballast tanks of a ship from Asia and has today spread to some European rivers?
 (a) Chinese Crab
 (b) Gonaxis
 (c) Walking Catfish
 (d) Giant Toad

160. Which animal was introduced into Jamaica from India in 1872 to control the rat population there?
 (a) Snake
 (b) Mongoose
 (c) Cat
 (d) Civet

IV

POLLUTION

General

161. 'The only thing free is _____.' Which word completes this popular expression that is no more valid today?
    (a) Water   (b) Air
    (c) Fire   (d) Soil

162. Since the widespread use of DDT, which effect has been observed in birds?
    (a) Fewer feathers (b) Thinner eggshells
    (c) Blindness   (d) Stunted growth

163. What is the major route for the widespread distribution of more persistent pesticides?
    (a) Soil
    (b) Water
    (c) Living organisms
    (d) Atmosphere

164. The higher the elevation of a town above the sea level, the larger the dose of something the human population is exposed to. What is it?

(a) Nuclear radiation
(b) Cosmic rays
(c) Electromagnetic radiations
(d) All

165. Who remarked, 'It is unfortunate, but true, that pollution is not just a technical problem, as was the case of putting man on the Moon. It is as much sociological as technological'?
(a) Thomas Jefferson
(b) Jared Elliot
(c) Jimmy Carter
(d) Lee. A.Du Bridge

166. Which is a first-rate pollution monitor?
(a) Mollusc   (b) Honey bee
(c) Dandelion   (d) Butterfly

167. It has been estimated that the molecules of a pesticide like DDT may remain intact in ecosystems for several years. How many years?
(a) 100 years   (b) 50 years
(c) 25 years   (d) 10 years

168. The concentration of DDT has been the maximum in the breast muscles of birds that eat this. What is it?
(a) Flesh   (b) Fish

(c) Plant   (d) All

169. Which source of sound can rupture the eardrum, damage the lungs and destroy property?
    (a) Electric train (b) Supersonic aircraft
    (c) Textile factory (d) None

170. Who said, 'You may forgive noise but your arteries never will'?
    (a) Robert McCarrison
    (b) Fritjof Capra
    (c) Samuel Rosen
    (d) Miriam Rothschild

171. The thoughtless dumping of this gadget into the environment has created a potential hazard to ecology and life in recent times. What is it?
    (a) Television
    (b) Computer
    (c) Refrigerator
    (d) Mobile phone

Daily Life

172. Which metal found in the atmosphere of roads heavy with traffic affects health adversely?
    (a) Cadmium   (b) Lead

(c) Chromium (d) Zinc

173. Which activity of the modern man sets the nitrate time-bomb ticking?
    (a) Farming (b) Tanning
    (c) Washing (d) Mining

174. Which type of landscape is often treated as a wasteland suitable only for dumping rubbish and sewage or reclamation but is biologically highly productive?
    (a) Mountains (b) Rocky terrain
    (c) Scrubland (d) Wetland

175. Whatever water is used at home gets polluted. Which household activity pollutes water the most?
    (a) Toilet-cleaning
    (b) Washing and bathing
    (c) Dish-washing
    (d) Drinking and cooking

176. Which gas found frequently in the air of roads with heavy traffic, especially underground tunnels and garages, affects health adversely?
    (a) Carbon dioxide
    (b) Ozone
    (c) Carbon monoxide
    (d) Sulphur dioxide

177. Lichens have disappeared from cities because they are highly susceptible to this gas. What is it?
    (a) Carbon dioxide (b) Nitrogen
    (c) Nitric oxide (d) Sulphur dioxide

178. Which source of noise is painful to hear and may lead to loss of hearing?
    (a) Rock and roll music
    (b) Subway train
    (c) Motorcycle
    (d) Mixer

179. A newspaper contains one toxic element. What is it?
    (a) Cadmium (b) Lead
    (c) Manganese (d) Mercury

180. When does a motor car produce the minimum amount of pollution?
    (a) Idling (b) Moving
    (c) Accelerating (d) Decelerating

181. As innocuous activity as a hair-spraying, can on a large scale, drastically affect this. What is it?
    (a) Ozone layer
    (b) Ionosphere
    (c) Magnetosphere
    (d) Troposphere

182. Which is the extreme cause of noise pollution?
    (a) Sonic booms produced by aircraft
    (b) Noise produced by industrial operations
    (c) Noise produced by traffic
    (d) Rock music

Indoor Pollution

183. Which is the major source of harmful radiations at home?
    (a) Tubelight   (b) Colour TV
    (c) Microwave oven (d) Heater

184. The poisonous gas carbon monoxide can reach hazardous levels in specifically located houses. Which ones?
    (a) Adjacent to garages
    (b) Crowded together
    (c) Skyscrapers
    (d) Near an industry

185. Coal-burning hearths or stoves produce one hazardous gas. Which one?
    (a) Sulphur dioxide
    (b) Carbon dioxide
    (c) Carbon monoxide
    (d) Hydrogen sulphide

186. Which is the largest source of the pollutant, formaldehyde vapour, in a room?
    (a) Utensils   (b) Furniture
    (c) Cooking range (d) Books

187. Both nitrogen dioxide and carbon monoxide are found in higher amounts in homes having this. What is it?
    (a) Gas cookers
    (b) Fire hearths
    (c) Wooden furniture
    (d) All

188. Photocopying and other electrical equipment produce one pollutant. Which one?
    (a) Methane
    (b) Ozone
    (c) Hydrogen sulphide
    (d) Nitrogen dioxide

189. Which harmful gas is emitted by masonry building materials, even groundwater?
    (a) Hydrogen sulphide (b) Radon
    (c) Ammonia   (d) Carbon dioxide

190. Which chemical is present in ordinary tap water?
    (a) Barium   (b) Chromium
    (c) Flourine (d) Chlorine

191. What do gas cookers cause?
    (a) Eye illnesses
    (b) Mental illnesses
    (c) Nasal illnesses
    (d) Respiratory illnesses

192. What is it that smoking produces in the largest amount?
    (a) Nitrogen oxide
    (b) Carbon monoxide
    (c) Particulate matter
    (d) Carbon dioxide

193. Ceramic crockery, if not fired at high enough temperatures, could become a source of pollutant in food taken in it. Which is that pollutant?
    (a) Cadmium   (b) Lead
    (c) Chromium   (d) Mercury

Air-borne Pollution

194. How do air pollutants enter the body?
    (a) Respiratory system
    (b) Digestive system
    (c) Excretory system
    (d) All

195. Which pollutant gas is released by cud-chewing domestic animals?

(a) Methane
(b) Carbon dioxide
(c) Carbon monoxide
(d) Nitrogen dioxide

196. In a photochemical smog, which gas is the principal eye and mucous-membrane irritant?
(a) Sulphur dioxide
(b) Ozone
(c) Carbon monoxide
(d) Nitrous oxide

197. Electrostatic scrubbers meant to absorb pollutants produce one pollutant. Which one?
(a) Sulphur dioxide
(b) Carbon monoxide
(c) Dust
(d) Ozone

198. Which pollutant gas has adversely affected the once prosperous flower-growing industry in Los Angeles, USA?
(a) Sulphur dioxide
(b) Carbon dioxide
(c) Ozone
(d) Nitrous oxide

199. What generates fly ash–the environmental pollutant?
    (a) Thermal power plant
    (b) Oil refinery
    (c) Fertiliser plant
    (d) Strip mining

200. Which gas can suffocate living beings to death?
    (a) Carbon dioxide
    (b) Carbon monoxide
    (c) Hydrogen sulphide
    (d) Sulphur dioxide

201. Which gas is mainly responsible for the creation of the Greenhouse Effect?
    (a) Ozone   (b) Oxygen
    (c) Carbon dioxide (d) Carbon monoxide

202. Which is the most abundant of all the hydrocarbon pollutants in the atmosphere?
    (a) Propane   (b) Methane
    (c) Butane   (d) Benzene

203. Which pollutant gas does a landfill produce?
    (a) Methane
    (b) Ammonia
    (c) Hydrogen sulphide
    (d) Sulphur dioxide

Water-borne Pollution

204. Which oil-tanker accident first alerted the public of the grave problem of oil spills in oceans?
    (a) *Agro Merchant* (b) *Ocean Eagle*
    (c) *Exxon Valdez* (d) *Torrey Canyon*

205. The mussels and oysters of this sea are unsafe to eat. Which sea is it?
    (a) Arabian sea
    (b) Caribbean sea
    (c) Mediterranean sea
    (d) Yellow sea

206. Which regions of seas and oceans are the most polluted?
    (a) Estuarine   (b) Coastal
    (c) Sea depths   (d) Coral reefs

207. What percentage of pollution in seas and oceans is contributed by land-based activities?
    (a) About 56%   (b) About 28%
    (c) About 83%   (d) About 95%

208. Which is the gas that produces the most damaging acid rains?
    (a) Sulphur dioxide
    (b) Nitrous oxide

(c) Carbon dioxide
(d) Hydrogen

209. Which type of nuclear bomb was tested on a Pacific atoll?
(a) Atom bomb   (b) Hydrogen bomb
(c) Neutron bomb (d) None

210. Which river was known till recently as 'Europe's industrial sewer'?
(a) Lena   (b) Rhine
(c) Rhine   (d) Amur

211. When were the old-fashioned soaps gradually replaced by synthetic detergents leading to enormous water pollution?
(a) After 1945   (b) After 1920
(c) After 1890   (d) After 1980

212. Human activities speed up the eutrophication process of this. What is it?
(a) Stream   (b) Lake
(c) River   (d) Sea

213. Which are the chemicals that fertilisers wash out into the water supply in large amounts?
(a) Nitrites   (b) Sulphates
(c) Nitrates   (d) Carbonates

214. What is the recent source of pollution of underground water?

(a) Landfills
(b) Sewers
(c) Biogas plants
(d) Thermal power stations

Nuclear Pollution

215. Which class of beings is least sensitive to nuclear radiations?
    (a) Single-celled organisms
    (b) Amphibians
    (c) Reptiles
    (d) Birds

216. For every kilowatt of power generated, a nuclear plant produces on an average this much more heat than a coal-fired plant. How much?
    (a) 20%   (b)   30%
    (c) 40%   (d)   50%

217. Nuclear radiations can cause a disease to the eyes when exposed to them. Which one?
    (a) Retinitis   (b) Cataract
    (c) Trachoma   (d) All

218. Which harmful substance released in the fallout of a nuclear explosion has the longest life?

(a) Iodine-131
(b) Cesium-137
(c) Strontium-89
(d) Plutonium-239

219. The main danger posed by a nuclear reactor is the release of harmful fission products into this. What is it?
(a) Steam   (b) Water
(c) Air   (d) All

220. Which nuclear radiation is harmful to the body from the outside?
(a) Gamma rays   (b) X-rays
(c) Neutron rays (d) All

221. Which is the major pollution problem blocking the further growth of the nuclear power industry?
(a) Disposal of nuclear waste
(b) Reactor safety
(c) Leakage of nuclear pollutants
(d) Health of the personnel

222. Which isotope released by a nuclear explosion is of the greatest concern to human health?
(a) Cesium-137   (b) Iodine-131
(c) Strontium-90 (d) None

223. Which class of beings is the most sensitive to nuclear radiations?
    (a) Mammals   (b) Amphibians
    (c) Reptiles   (d) Birds

V

HAZARDS AND DISEASES

Professional Hazards

224. Scrotal skin cancer occurs due to heavy exposure to soot. Who were the first to be afflicted?
    (a) Chimney sweepers
    (b) Smelter workers
    (c) Coal miners
    (d) Refinery workers

225. Which industry's workers suffer from 'Byssinosis'?
    (a) Cardboard   (b) Paper
    (c) Plastics   (d) Textile

226. Who are afflicted with 'Black lung' disease?
    (a) Farmers
    (b) Coal miners
    (c) Quarry workers
    (d) Refinery workers

227. Which type of workers suffer more frequently from cancer?
    (a) Uranium miners

    (b) Coal miners
    (c) Sailors
    (d) Truck drivers

228. Which type of woman workers were first to die of cancer from exposure to nuclear radiations?
    (a) Assemblers of colour-TV receivers
    (b) Painters of luminous watch dials
    (c) Nurses handling X-ray machines
    (d) Air hostesses

229. Which class of workers is exposed to higher levels of radiation than the normal population?
    (a) Railway engine drivers
    (b) Hovercraft crew
    (c) Anti-aircraft personnel
    (d) Aircraft crew

230. Who died of Leukaemia caused by radioactivity while experimenting with its effects?
    (a) Pierre Curie
    (b) Marie Curie
    (c) Henri Becquerel
    (d) Irene Joliot-Curie

231. Workers suffer from 'Asbestosis' when they inhale this material while cutting, crushing

and sanding it. What is it?
(a) Plastics
(b) Coal
(c) Asbestos
(d) PCBs

232. In industries in which concentrations of toxic compounds are often higher than the outside environment, workers mostly suffer from diseases involving this. Which one?
(a) Brain   (b) Ears
(c) Skin   (d) Bones

233. Who suffer from space sickness or space adaptation syndrome?
(a) Aircraft pilots (b) Astronauts
(c) Sailors   (d) Deep-sea divers

Diseases

234. What is responsible for more cases of human illness the world over than any other environmental factor?
(a) Air pollution   (b) Water pollution
(c) Soil pollution   (d) Deforestation

235. Which deadly disease spreads with the expansion of agriculture?
(a) Cholera   (b) Rabies

(c) Kala-azar   (d) Malaria

236. Which of the following's presence in the air causes allergic reactions in some individuals?
(a) Talcum powder (b) Hair spray
(c) Hair dye   (d) House dust

237. Which disease occurs in children less than one year old who have insufficient food?
(a) Diarrhoea   (b) Marasmus
(c) Kwashiorkar   (d) Measles

238. What has sudden and unexpected noise been found to do?
(a) Increase the blood pressure
(b) Increase the heart rate
(c) Produce muscular contractions
(d) All

239. Which disease is associated with the felling of forests?
(a) Dengue
(b) Actinomycosis
(c) Kayasanur forest disease
(d) All

240. What do harmful ultraviolet radiations coming from the sun cause?
(a) Liver cancer   (b) Skin cancer
(c) Mouth cancer   (d) Lung cancer

241. Which disease occurs in one-to-four-year-old children due to a protein-deficient diet?
    (a) Whooping cough
    (b) Kwashiorkar
    (c) Diptheria
    (d) Tetanus

242. People contract hay fever form the presence of one pollutant in the air. Which one?
    (a) House dust   (b) Pollen
    (c) Talcum powder (d) Hair spray

243. Which disease has spread in Egypt as a result of the impoundment of the Nile river behind Aswan dam?
    (a) *Helminthiasis* (b) *Schistosomiasis*
    (c) *Dermatomycosis* (d) *Colitis*

Chemicals and Diseases

244. Whose dust causes 'Fibrosis' in lungs?
    (a) Silica
    (b) Asbestos
    (c) Chlorinated hydrocarbons
    (d) Lead

245. Which metal was responsible for the fatal brain disease that afflicted people eating fish caught around Minamata off the

Japanese island Kyushu?

(a) Lead   (b) Copper

(c) Manganese   (d) Mercury

246. Which element is a carcinogen or cancer-producing agent?

(a) Chromium   (b) Cadmium

(c) Ammonia   (d) Carbon

247. What does excessive inhalation of manganese cause?

(a) Anaemia   (b) Diptheria

(c) Pneumonia   (d) Gout

248. Which chemical is a mutagen or mutation-causing agent?

(a) Chlorinated hydrocarbons

(b) Organophosphates

(c) Nitrogen oxides

(d) Epoxy resins

249. Where did the epidemic bone-softening disease 'Itai-Itai' occur as a result of the presence of cadmium in the environment?

(a) Myanmar   (b) Thailand

(c) South Korea   (d) Japan

250. Which metal causes systemic poisoning in man?

(a) Zinc

(b) Manganese

(c) Selenium   (d) Lead

251. Whose dust causes 'Silicosis'?
   (a) Silicon dioxide
   (b) Silica
   (c) Sulphur dioxide
   (d) Sulphur

252. Which of the following elements is a carcinogen or cancer-producing agent in man?
   (a) Arsenic   (b) Gold
   (c) Calcium   (d) All

253. Which disease in children is caused by the intensive use of nitrate fertilisers?
   (a) Mumps
   (b) Jaundice
   (c) Septicaemia
   (d) Methemoglobinemia

VI

PORTRAIT QUIZ

254. Obviously, this lady is a biologist. And she is the most famous person in environmental science. Who is she?

255. This lady is a great lover of gibbons. Who is she?

256. He is renowned for paintings of birds. Who is he?

257. With binoculars and a rifle hanging around his neck, this old man was a conservator of a wild animal. Who is he?

258. He is India's leading ecologist and conservationist, who has done pioneering work linking biodiversity and the needs of communities and poor people. Who is he?

259. A supreme court advocate, he has successfully fought for the creation of appropriate environmental laws in India. Who is he?

260. He has set up a snake park in Chennai. Who is he?

VII

CRUCIAL MILIEUS

Oceans

261. Who remarked, 'We treat the ocean as if we believed that it is not part of our own world, as if the blue water curved into space some where beyond the horizon and our pollutants would fall off the edge, as ships were believed to do before the days of Christopher Columbus...'?
    (a) Jacques-Yves Cousteau
    (b) Wesley Marx
    (c) Thor Heyerdahl
    (d) John Clark

262. Which is the deepest spot in an ocean?
    (a) Atacama Trench, Pacific
    (h) Tuscarora Deep, Pacific
        Ceara Abyssal Plain, Atlantic
    (d) Mariana Trench, Pacific

263. Which is the mathematically constructed spiral that describes the effect of wind on the ocean?

(a) Archimedean spiral
(b) Ekman spiral
(c) Logarithmic spiral
(d) All

264. When did the United Nations put into force the Law of the Sea?
(a) 1962　　　　(b) 1972
(c) 1952　　　　(d) 1982

265. Which regions of oceans and seas are mined for petroleum?
(a) Estuaries　　(b) Continental shelves
(c) Trenches　　(d) All

266. Ecologically, how many regions is an ocean divided into?
(a) Two regions　(b) Five regions
(c) Eight regions (d) Three regions

267. What is the origin of an atoll?
(a) Volcano　　　(b) Trench
(c) Rift valley　　(d) All

268. What is the occasional, rhythmic rise and fall of water in closed lagoons or bays known as?
(a) Seiche
(b) Rossby waves
(c) Surfbeat
(d) Internal waves

269. What is the charting of the ocean floor by taking soundings called?
    (a) Bathymetry   (b) SONAR
    (c) SOFAR   (d) Bathyscape

270. Which vessel is a drilling ship?
    (a) *HMS Challenger* (b) *Finn Polaris*
    (c) *Gaveshani*   (d) *Glomar Challenger*

271. What is the average depth of oceans?
    (a) 2,610 metres   (b) 3,730 metres
    (c) 4,840 metres   (d) 5,620 metres

272. Which ocean is slowly expanding due to continental drift?
    (a) Pacific Ocean   (b) Indian Ocean
    (c) Atlantic Ocean (d) Arctic Ocean

273. Which of the following seas is essentially a lake?
    (a) Caspian Sea   (b) Jawa Sea
    (c) Red Sea   (d) Black Sea

274. Which oceanic region's current direction is dependent upon the monsoon?
    (a) Bay of Bengal (b) Bering Sea
    (c) Caribbean Sea (d) Chesapeak Bay

275. Where do manganese nodules, the potential source of minerals in oceans, form?
    (a) On the continental shelves

(b) Trenches with circular current

(c) Lagoons with still waters

(d) Ocean beds with mild current

276. Where is the coral reef belt located?
    (a) Pacific Ocean
    (b) Between 30N and 30S latitude
    (c) Between10N and 10S latitude
    (d) About the Equator

Space

277. For the first time, amino acids, basic ingredients of living matter, were found in a meteorite fall. Where did the meteorite fall?
    (a) Murchison, Australia
    (b) Prince George, Canada
    (c) Kilrea, Ireland
    (d) Ibadan, Nigeria

278. Which is the faint glow visible in the night sky exactly opposite to the direction of sun?
    (a) Zodiacal light
    (b) *Gegenschein*
    (c) Green flash
    (d) Air-glow

279. Tiny glass objects are found in certain parts of the world and are believed to have their origin in the Moon. What are they?
(a) Chrondites   (b) Geminids
(c) Aerolites   (d) Tektites

280. Which planet is often described as a cold, lifeless desert?
(a) Saturn   (b) Jupiter
(c) Mercury   (d) Mars

281. Which terrestrial sphere extends into space?
(a) Ecosphere   (b) Biosphere
(c) Exosphere   (d) Magnetosphere

282. What is the origin of meteor showers that occur in certain months of the year regularly?
(a) Dead comets   (b) Meteoroids
(c) Both   (d) Neither

283. Which planet is believed to have the 'Runaway Greenhouse effect'?
(a) Mars   (b) Earth
(c) Venus   (d) Jupiter

284. Which animal was the first to enter space and indicate that life can exist in it?
(a) Monkey   (b) Dog
(c) Cat   (d) Mouse

285. What causes magnetic storms?

(a) Solar wind   (b) Nitrogen

(c) Water   (d) Sodium chloride

286. Which is the most precious commodity on earth not yet found on any other planet of the solar system?

(a) Hydrogen sulphide

(b) Nitrogen

(c) Water

(d) Comet debris

287. What kind of pollution presently threatens the space beyond the earth?

(a) Space junk   (b) Meteoroids

(c) Radiation   (d) Comet debris

Atmosphere

288. Which is the hot, dry sand-land wind what blows from Africa to the Mediterranean region?

(a) Fohn   (b) Sirocco

(c) Loo   (d) Monsoon

289. Lightning discharges affect one nature's cycle. Which one?

(a) Carbon cycle

(b) Sulphur cycle

(c) Phosphorus cycle

(d) Nitrogen cycle

290. Which is the long, narrow current of high speed winds that blow at high altitudes?
(a) Jet stream   (b) Gulf stream
(c) Van Allen belts (d) Kuroshio current

291. Which is the atmospheric layer where temperature of the air increases with height?
(a) Mesosphere   (b) Troposphere
(c) Stratosphere   (d) All

292. Which atmospheric phenomenon is directly linked to the oceanic phenomenon of El Nino?
(a) Jet streams   (b) Clouds
(c) Southern oscillation   (d) Rainbow

293. Breezes in coastal areas are caused by the difference in something between air over land and sea. What is it?
(a) Pressure   (b) Temperature
(c) Humidity   (d) All

294. Which natural phenomenon can carry precious top-soil for hundreds of kilometres?
(a) Dust storms   (b) Clouds
(c) Rains   (d) Cyclones

295. Where is dust dome, a haze of smoke and dust that forms an umbrella over a region, seen?

(a) City   (b) Village
(c) Lake   (d) Mountains

296. Which meteorological phenomenon helps build up levels of pollutants in atmosphere instead of dispersing them?
(a) Lightning   (b) Rain
(c) Rainbow   (d) Thermal inversion

297. Which acid does normal rain contain in a dilute form?
(a) Sulphuric acid
(b) Nitric acid
(c) Hydrochloric acid
(d) Carbonic acid

Forests

298. Which type of forest is the most fertile reservoir of wildlife?
(a) Temperate forest
(b) Tropical rainforest
(c) Boreal forest
(d) All

299. Which type of forest is least likely to be destroyed by fire, natural or man-made?
(a) Deciduous forest
(b) Coniferous forest

(c) Broad-leaf evergreen forest
(d) Rainforest

300. Where is one-third of all the world's rainforest located?
(a) India   (b) China
(c) Brazil   (d) Zaire

301. The management of a forest becomes difficult mainly due to this. What is this?
(a) The society that lives off it.
(b) The peculiar ecology.
(c) The presence of big animals.
(d) The peculiar behaviour of some species of animals and birds.

302. What does deforestation lead to?
(a) Diminishing rainfall
(b) Less reliable water supplies
(c) Soil erosion and siltation in rivers
(d) All

303. The floor of a rain forest is covered by a thin layer of this. What is it?
(a) Water
(b) Subsoil water
(c) Animal debris
(d) Plant debris

304. Most of the forest the worldover has been or is being damaged by this. What is it?

(a) Air-borne pollutants
(b) Water-borne pollutants
(c) Acid rains
(d) Soil-borne pollutants

305. Where is the largest rain forest in the world located?
 (a) Amazon basin (b) Congo basin
 (c) Indonesia (d) Philippines

306. How many types of forest fires are there?
 (a) Two (b) Three
 (c) Four (d) None

307. Rainforests are being destroyed largely due to this. What is it?
 (a) Ignorance (b) Greed
 (c) Poverty (d) Stupidity

308. Destruction of forests and denudation of vegetation will change one parameter of the earth. Which one?
 (a) Albedo (b) Shape
 (c) Heat budget (d) Radiations budget

309. Who said, 'A nation's wealth, its real wealth, can be gauged by its tree cover'?
 (a) Sundarlal Bahuguna
 (b) Shivram Karanth
 (c) Chico Mendes
 (d) Richard St Barbe Baker

Fields

310. Where did agriculture originate?
     - (a) South America
     - (b) Western Asia
     - (c) Northeastern Africa
     - (d) All

311. Of the 2000 varieties of rice that were once cultivated around the world, hardly 25 of them are today grown due to this. What is it?
     - (a) The White Revolution
     - (b) The Communication Revolution
     - (c) The Green Revolution
     - (d) The Information Revolution

312. What is known as a 'Miracle crop'?
     - (a) Sunflower   (b) Corn
     - (c) Soyabean   (d) Tobacco

313. Where was the terrace type of agriculture developed?
     - (a) The Philippines
     - (b) Thailand
     - (c) Peru
     - (d) China

314. A plant needs a number of chemical elements for its growth. How many?
(a) 10   (b) 16
(c) 22   (d) 5

315. When were synthetic fertilisers first manufactured on a large scale and used in agriculture?
(a) the 1910s   (b) the 1920s
(c) the 1930s   (d) the 1950s

316. Which ancient civilisation developed floating gardens for agriculture?
(a) Aztec   (b) Indus
(c) Babylonia   (d) All

317. What is the estimated percentage of the world's land suitable for farming?
(a) 12   (b) 24
(c) 32   (d) 8

318. Where did swidden-slash and burn farming originate?
(a) South America (b)   Europe
(c) Africa   (d)   Australia

319. Which is the truly domesticated grain entirely dependent on man for its survival?
(a) Rice   (b) Maize
(c) Barley   (d) Wheat

VIII
MOVEMENTS AND SUCCESSES

Movements

320. Who originally inspired the environment movement?
     (a) Jean Jacques Rousseau
     (b) Henry David Thoreau
     (c) Robert Owen
     (d) Rachel Carson

321. Who formed the backbone of the Indian ecological movement, the Chipko movement?
     (a) Forest Department
     (b) Women
     (c) Students
     (d) Sarvodaya leaders

322. Which harmful item was discussed at length in Rachel Carson's *Silent Spring*, whose effect on environment triggered off the environment awareness movement the world over?

(a) PCB (b) Carbon dioxide
(c) Freon (d) DDT

323. When was the Jawaharlal Nehru Community Biodiversity movement launched in India?
(a) 1988 (b) 1989
(c) 1969 (d) 1985

324. Which mass movement is in full swing, especially in the developed countries?
(a) Green consumer (b) Chipko
(c) Anti-nuclear (d) Tree plantation

325. Where was the *Mitti bachao* (Save the soil) movement launched in India.
(a) Thane, Maharashtra
(b) Mysore, Karnataka
(c) Darbhanga, Bihar
(d) Hoshangabad, M.P.

326. Which country has the oldest tradition of popular movements aimed at the protection of natural and man-made environment?
(a) Italy
(b)   The United Kingdom
(c) Japan
(d) Sweden

327. Which body pioneered the *Chipko* movement?

(a) Dasohli Gram Swarajya Mandal
(b) Vana Raksha Parished
(c) Gandhi Peace Foundation
(d) Friends of the Tree Society

328. Where is the 'Green Belt Movement' organised by women in progress?
(a) New Zealand   (b) Kenya
(c) India   (d) China

329. Where did the *Appiko* movement start in India?
(a) Kerala   (b) Madhya Pardesh
(c) Andhra Pardesh(d) Karnataka

Success Stories

330. Which country declared itself a nuclear-free zone in 1984 in response to a successful anti-nuclear movement?
(a) Canada   (b) Australia
(c) Switzerland   (d) New Zealand

331. Which species of seal taken to be extinct for almost a century was rediscovered on an island off the coast of Chile?
(a) Ross Seal   (b) Elephant Seal
(c) Hooded Seal
(d) Juan Fernandez Seal

332. Which bird has today been brought back from the edge of extinction and has as a result become a symbol of resurgence and hope for all endangered species?
   (a) Dodo
   (b) Sage Grouse
   (c) Nene
   (d) Andean Condor

333. Which animal — extinct long ago in Russia — was re-introduced in the country and is now flourishing?
   (a) Reindeer
   (b) Brown Bear
   (c) Musk Ox
   (d) Caribou

334. Which rare buttercup, almost given up as lost for some time, has proliferated as a result of a change in the management of its reserve?
   (a) Greater Spearwort
   (b) Meadow Buttercup
   (c) Lesser Spearwort
   (d) Adder's tongue Spearwort

335. Which Indian bird sanctuary was once the duck-shooting ground of a king?
   (a) Vedaranyam bird sanctuary
   (b) Bharatpur bird sanctuary
   (c) Ranganathittu
   (d) Point Calimere sanctuary

336. Which animal, almost on the verge of

extinction, was successfully bred in captivity and has been introduced in its desert habitat?

(a) Dorcas Gazelle
(b) Arabian Oryx
(c) South African Oryx
(d) None

337. Salmon was caught in this river after 60 years in 1974 when it was cleansed of pollution after intensive research. Which is the river?

(a) Ganga   (b) Thames
(c) Nile   (d) Angara

338. Which acacia-like tree, once found on Easter Island and thought to have become extinct, is now fast flourishing and is likely to be returned to its wild habitat?

(a) *Sophora japonica*
(b) *Robinia pseudoacacia*
(c) *Gleditisia triacanthus*
(d) *Sophara toromiro*

339. The hunting of this endangered bird by Arab Sheikhs was stopped in India in 1977 when wildlife lovers created an uproar. Which is the bird?

(a) Chir Pheasant

(c) Blacknecked Crane
(c) Bar-headed Goose
(d) Great Indian Bustard

340. Which animal once brought on the verge of extinction for its soft, warm wool by the Spanish conquistadores has been successfully bred in a reserve?
    (a) Axis Deer   (b) Andean Vicuna
    (c) Pronghorn   (d) White-tailed Deer

341. Which bird once massacred in large numbers for its tasty flesh, and become almost extinct, has managed to hang on to its small population as a result of the dedicated work of a single enthusiast?
    (a) Red Jungle Fowl
    (b) Red-breasted Goose
    (c) Cahow
    (d) Rock Partridge

342. Which was restored to normalcy from its eutrophified state?
    (a) Volta Lake   (b) Lake Nasser
    (c) Chilka Lake   (d) Lake Washington

IX

ESTABLISHMENTS

Institutes

343. Where is the G.B. Pant institute of Himalayan Environment and Development located?
    (a) Leh
    (b) Pithoragarh
    (c) Nainital
    (d) Almora

344. Where is the Asian Elephant Research and Conservation Centre located?
    (a) Kodaikanal
    (b) Mysore
    (c) Bangalore
    (d) Vijayawada

345. Where is the office of the 'Campaign for Clean Ganga' located?
    (a) Allahabad
    (b) Prayag
    (c) Varanasi
    (d) Haridwar

346. Where is the Salim Ali Centre for Ornithology located?
    (a) Coimbatore
    (b) Ratnagiri
    (c) Shillong
    (d) Almora

347. Where is the C.P. Ramaswami Aiyer Environmental Education Centre located?

(a) Chandigarh   (b) Cochin
(c) Bangalore   (d) Chennai

348. Where is the Centre for Environmental Studies located?
    (a) Chennai   (b) Cochin
    (c) Bangalore   (d) Chandigarh

349. Where is the National Environmental Engineering Research Institute located?
    (a) Kolkata   (b) Nagpur
    (c) Jorhat   (d) Shillong

Parks

350. Where is the Engadine National Park located?
    (a) Italy   (b) Peru
    (c) Switzerland   (d) Argentina

351. Where is the Tsavo Royal Park located?
    (a) New Zealand   (b) Myanmar
    (c) Brazil   (d) Kenya

352. Where is Khao Yai National Park located?
    (a) Japan   (b) Thailand
    (c) Myanmar   (d) Nepal

353. Where is the Chitwan National Park located?
    (a) Myanmar   (b) Malaysia
    (c) Nepal   (d) India

354. Where is the Kruger National Park located?
    (a) USA   (b) Canada
    (c) Germany   (d) South Africa

355. Where is the Bonaire Marine Park located ?
    (a) Caribbean Islands
    (b) New Zealand
    (c) Australia
    (d) Hawaii Islands

356. Where is the Murchison Falls Park located?
    (a) Uganda   (b) South Africa
    (c) Thailand   (d) Nepal

357. Where is the Serengeti National Park located?
    (a) Tanzania   (b) Sri Lanka
    (c) Myanmar   (d) Kenya

358. Where is the Oka National Park located?
    (a) Russia   (b) USA
    (c) Norway   (d) Australia

359. Where is the Albert Park located?
    (a) Zambia   (b) Congo
    (c) Pakistan   (d) Sri Lanka

360. Where is the man-made William Curtis
    Ecological Park, which gives an urbanite an
    idea of wildlife, located?
    (a) Paris   (b) London
    (c) Liverpool   (d) New York

X

MEDIA AND AWARDS

Journals

361. Which colourful magazine on nature is brought out by the American Museum of Natural History?
    (a) *National Geographic*
    (b) *Natural History*
    (c) *Nature*
    (d) *Nature and Resources*

362. Which Indian body bring out *Bhagirath*, a journal devoted to water resources?
    (a) Central Water Commission
    (b) Indian Meteorological Organization
    (c) National Institute of Oceanography
    (d) None

363. Which university in the USA brings out the *Ecology Law Quarterly*?
    (a) California
    (b) South Carolina
    (c) IIlinois
    (d) Wisconsin

364. Which journal does the American Society for Environmental History bring out?
(a) *Environmental Review*
(b) *Environmental Research*
(c) *Environment*
(d) *Ecologist*

365. Who is the Editor of *Sanctuary Magazine*?
(a) Zafar Futehally
(b) Bittu Sehgal
(c) Dilip Mathews
(d) N. Krishnan

366. Which journal is brought out by the Institution of Environmental Sciences, London?
(a) *Urban Ecology*
(b) *Environmentalist*
(c) *Biocycle*
(d) *Ecology Abstracts*

367. Which journal is brought out by the Foundation for Environmental Conservation, Switzerland?
(a) *Environmental Action*
(b) *Environmental Research*
(c) *Ecology*
(d) *Environmental Conservation*

368. Which Indian institute or laboratory brings out the *Indian Journal of Environmental Health*?
    (a) National Environmental Engineering Research Institute
    (b) Industrial Toxicological Research Institute of Science
    (c) Indian Institute of Science
    (d) National Institute of Oceanography

369. Which organisation publishes Environmental Health Perspectives, a journal devoted to environment-related health issues?
    (a) National Institute of Environmental Health Sciences, USA
    (b) Indian Institute of Ecology and Environment, India
    (c) United Nations Environment Programme, Switzerland
    (d) Tata Energy Research Institute, India

370. Which organisation publishes the fortnightly *Down To Earth* that gives an up-to-date state of environment in India and the world?
    (a) Centre for Science and Environment
    (b) Kalpavriksha
    (c) National Environmental Engineering Research Institute
    (d) Tata Energy Research Institute

371. Which journal on human environment issues is brought out by the Royal Swedish Academy of Sciences?
    (a) *Parks*
    (b) *Ambio*
    (c) *The Sanctuary*
    (d) *Conservation News Service*

372. Which international organisation brings out the journal Nature and Resources?
    (a) WWF-N
    (b) IBPGR
    (c) IUCN
    (d) UNESCO

Films

373. Who has made the public at large, aware of oceans, their environment, and life through his films and TV serials?
    (a) Jacques-Yves Cousteau
    (b) Arthur C. Clarke
    (c) David Attenborough
    (d) Michael Cousteau

374. Who were the first to make a film on the life cycle of the *gharial*?
    (a) Armand Davis
    (b) Naresh and Rajesh Bedi
    (c) Alan Root
    (d) Marlin Perkins

375. Who made the controversial film *On the Edge of the Forests*?
    (a) Richard St. Barbie Baker
    (b) E.F. Schumacher
    (c) Lee Durrell
    (d) Sunderlal Bahuguna

376. Which film is based on the reports of the spread of a voracious species of bees crossbred between African killer bee and a South American species?
    (a) *The Bees*
    (b) *The Swarm*
    (c) *Return of the Fly*
    (d) *Lord of the Flies*

377. Serengeti is a place in Africa teeming with big, wild animals. Who wrote the book *Serengeti Shall Not Die*, which was later made into film?
    (a) George Schaller (b) Bernhardt Grzimek
    (c) Branch Rickey (d) Armand Denis

378. Who made the film *Whistling Hunters*?
    (a) Marty Stouffer
    (b) Naresh and Rajesh Bedi
    (c) Andre Singer
    (d) Lee Durrell

379. Which actress led demonstrations against

the annual shooting of turtledoves during their migratory flight over the French town Medoc?

(a) Virginia McKenna
(b) Julie Andrews
(c) Elizabeth Taylor
(d) Brigitte Bardot

380. Which film depicted the scenes of a nuclear holocaust?

(a) *The Day After*
(b) *China Syndrome*
(c) *The Day the Earth Stood Still*
(d) *Doomswatch*

381. Which Indian heroine walked out of a film because it involved cruelty to animals?

(a) Shabana Azmi   (b) Sharmila Tagore
(c) Smita Patil   (d) Amala

382. Who made the documentary film *The Lions Are Free* which showed how lions in captivity are trained to live in the wild?

(a) Bernhardt Grzimek
(b) Bill Travers
(c) George Schaller
(d) Wolfgang Bayer

383. What does the movie *The Towering Inferno* deal with?

(a) Tornado disaster
(b) Nuclear holocaust
(c) Skyscraper disaster
(d) Dinosaur death

Awards

384. Which international body awards the International Environment Prize?
    (a) United Nations
    (b) World Resources Institute
    (c) Amnesty International
    (d) Earth Resources Research Institute

385. Which prize is offered by the US Smithsonian Institution for contributions to environmental studies, both from scientific and social points of view?
    (a) Audobon Medal
    (b) Hodgkins Medal and Prize
    (c) Edward J. Meeman Conservation Prize
    (d) Earthcare Prize

386. Which medal is presented every three years for distinguished service in conservation by the International Union for the Conservation of Nature and Natural Resources?
    (a) Audobon Medal
    (b) Carson Medal

(c) John C. Phillips Medal

(d) Aldo Leopold Memorial Medal

387. Which medal is conferred on a naturalist for his or her book on its literary and scientific contents?

(a) Rachel Carson Medal

(b) Audobon Medal

(c) Burroughs Medal

(d) Alexander von Humboldt Medal

388. Which Indian institution gives the Indira Priyadarshini Vrikshamitra Awards for contributions to wasteland development and afforestation?

(a) Department of Environment, Forests and Wildlife

(b) Department of Non-conventional Energy Sources

(c) Indian Forests Research Institute

(d) All

389. Which award is given for conservation by the Ecological Society of America?

(a) Rachel Carson Award

(b) MacArther Award

(c) Greenworld Award

(d) Earthcare Award

390. Which prize is given to an individual or organisation by the World Wide Fund for Nature for distinguished services to wildlife conservation?
    (a) Aldo Leopold Prize
    (b) Greenworld Prize
    (c) Earthcare Prize
    (d) J. Paul Getty Wildlife Conservation Prize

391. Which medal is conferred on an engineer for distinguished achievements in conservation by the US National Audobon Society?
    (a) Audobon Medal
    (b) Palladium Medal
    (c) Aldo Leopold Memorial Medal
    (d) John C. Phillips Medal

392. Which institution awards the Pitambar Pant National Environment fellowships?
    (a) Department of Science & Technology
    (b) Department of Non-Conventional Energy Sources
    (c) Department of Environment
    (d) Wildlife Institute of India

XI

IMPORTANT DATES

Treaties and Conventions

393. When was the Outer Space Treaty which prohibited the placing of nuclear or other weapons of mass destruction in orbit around the earth signed?
    (a) 1967   (b) 1956
    (c) 1970   (d) 1982

394. When was it agreed at an international meet that the use of poisonous gases in warfare would be banned?
    (a) 1930   (b) 1925
    (c) 1956   (d) 1948

395. When was the Threshold Test Ban Treaty limiting the size of nuclear weapon test explosions to 150 kilotons signed?
    (a) 1962   (b) 1968
    (c) 1974   (d) 1978

396. When was the International Convention for the Protection of Birds signed?
    (a) 1955   (b) 1960

(c) 1950   (d) 1965

397. When was the Sea-Bed Treaty, which prohibits the emplacement of nuclear weapons on the sea-bed beyond a 20 km zone, signed?
(a) 1972   (b) 1978
(c) 1971   (d) 1968

398. When was the RAMSAR convention on Wetlands f International Importance signed?
(a) 1956   (b) 1971
(c) 1962   (d) 1988

399. When was the Biological Weapons Convention prohibiting biological means of warfare signed?
(a) 1962   (b) 1975
(c) 1957   (d) 1972

400. Which two countries signed the Great Lakes Treaty in 1971 with the aim of saving their respective lakes from ecological disasters?
(a) The United States and Canada
(b) Sweden and the United Kingdom
(c) Norway and Sweden
(d) Norway and the United Kingdom

401. When was the Non-Proliferation Treaty, which prohibits the transfer of nuclear weapons by nuclear states, signed?

(a) 1970   (b) 1968
(c) 1984   (d) 1955

402. When was the Antarctic Treaty, which declared that the icy continent shall be used for peaceful purposes, signed?
(a) 1970   (b) 1959
(c) 1961   (d) 1978

403. When was the Partial Test Ban Treaty, which banned the testing of nuclear weapons in the atmosphere, in outer space, and underwater, signed?
(a) 1978   (b) 1952
(c) 1965   (d) 1963

404. When was the Environment Modification Convention aimed at prohibiting countries from modifying environment during war held?
(a) 1977   (b) 1963
(c) 1967   (d) 1981

Significant Events

405. When was the Campaign for Nuclear Disarmament started?
(a) 1982   (b) 1958
(c) 1951   (d) 1964

406. When did the Bhopal Gas Tragedy occur?
    (a) 1956   (b) 1984
    (c) 1980   (d) 1986

407. When were the seeds of high-yielding varieties of wheat, which led to the Green Revolution, introduced in India?
    (a) 1950   (b) 1966
    (c) 1972   (d) 1975

408. When did DDT, the infamous pesticide, find wide spread use in the world?
    (a) the late 1920s   (b) the late 1930s
    (c) the late 1940s   (d) the late 1950s

409. When was the Suez Canal, which allowed marine life of the Red Sea to cross over to the Mediterranean and vice versa, opened?
    (a) 1920   (b) 1931
    (c) 1869   (d) 1823

410. When did the Chernobyl Nuclear Reactor disaster occur?
    (a) 1978   (b) 1986
    (c) 1980   (d) 1984

XII

HUMAN AFFAIRS

Policy and Politics

411. Which chemical has the International Maritime Organisation banned from disposal into the sea?
     (a) Plastics   (b) Fertilizers
     (c) Pesticides   (d) Petrol

412. The International Fur Trade Federation has banned the trade of fur of one type of leopard. Which one?
     (a) Clouded Leopard
     (b) Snow Leopard
     (c) Hunting Leopard
     (d) All

413. What is the 30% Club associated with?
     (a) Desert   (b) Estuary
     (c) Forest   (d) Acid rain

414. What was Greenpeace originally known as?
     (a) Greenearth
     (b) Don't Make a Wave

    (c) Change the World

    (d) Watch the Next Move

415. Which country has proposed that industrialised countries should allocate 0.1 per cent of their Gross National Product for a World Atmosphere Fund as a starting point?
    (a) Switzerland   (b) Denmark
    (c) Norway   (d) Canada

416. Who is the author of *Green Parties*, dealing with the politics of the green movement the world over?
    (a) Petra Kelly
    (b) Sara Parkin
    (c) Jonathan Porritt
    (d) F.E. Trainer

417. The idea that national security can no longer be confined to military power but must also be extended to include forests, watersheds, crop lands, genetic resources and other environmental factors, was first pointed out in this. What is it?
    (a) *The Brandt Report*
    (b) *The Brundtland Report*
    (c) *United Nations Environment Program*
    (d) *Global 2000 Report*

418. Which country has adopted the slogan: 'Whoever afforests the land will own the trees'?
    (a) Canada   (b) Denmark
    (c) China   (d) Bangladesh

419. What is the United Nations Conference on Environment and Development more popular as?
    (a) Earth Summit (b) Eco-Meet
    (c) Geo-Meet   (d) Initiative Earth

420. Which is the buzz-word among all governments of the world?
    (a) Sustainable Development
    (b) Eco-tourism
    (c) Both
    (d) None

421. Where was the World Summit on Sustainable Development held in 2002?
    (a) Manila, Thailand
    (b) Johannesburg, South Africa
    (c) Kathmandu, Nepal
    (d) New York, USA

422. What does the 'Kyoto Protocol' deal with?
    (a) Curbing Greenhouse gas emissions
    (b) Checking asbestos menace
    (c) Checking wildlife trade
    (d) Banning whale hunting

423. Nowadays, saving which of the following is the top priority of conservationists.
    (a) Tropical forests (b) Tundras
    (c) Lakes   (d) Prairies

424. How many kilometres into the sea does the Exclusive Economic Zone of a coastal country extend?
    (a) 20 kilometres (b) 100 kilometres
    (c) 200 kilometres (d) 300 kilometres

425. Which country banned in 1989 the manufacture, use, and export of most asbestos products?
    (a) Russia   (b) Norway
    (c) USA   (d) Sweden

426. Which Green Party leader created the famous slogan: 'We are neither left nor right; we are in front'?
    (a) Stephanie Leland
    (b) Herbert Gruhl
    (c) Petra Kelly
    (d) Anonymous

427. Who was the first to use the slogan 'Our Spaceship Earth' during the US Presidential election?
    (a) George Bush   (b) Richard Nixon
    (c) Adlai Stevenson (d) John F. Kennedy

Culture

428. The level to which a culture can develop is dependent upon the potentiality of the environment it occupies. Which word will complete this proposition?
    (a) Technological (b) Agricultural
    (c) Scientific (d) Climatic

429. Which tree's stalks are often used by the Hindus for performing marriage and religious rites?
    (a) Banana (b) Tamarind
    (c) Mango (d) Kadamba

430. Which belief is mainly responsible for bringing the rhinoceros on the verge of extinction?
    (a) The horn has medicinal value.
    (b) The horn has ornamental value.
    (c) The horn has aphrodisiac value.
    (d) The horn makes very superior quality of perfume.

431. Which tree's leaves are used by the Hindus to decorate marriage pandals?
    (a) Temple Tree (b) Coral Jasmine
    (c) Ebony (d) Mango

432. Which type of environment has come to represent modernity?

(a) Forest   (b) Ocean
(c) Space   (d) Wilderness

433. Land is worshipped before the initiation of construction activities to ensure the integrity and importance of land. Which community of people perform this worship?
(a) The Hindus   (b) The Muslims
(c) The Jews   (d) The Parsis

434. Which colour has become established as a sign of conservation and environment?
(a) Orange   (b) Purple
(d) Saffron   (d) Green

435. Which tree is considered sacred by the Hindus and is seldom cut?
(a) Tulip Tree   (b) Coconut Palm
(c) Jujube Tree   (d) Peepal

436. Which animal is popular as the 'Doctor of the Arabs' in its native place?
(a) Camel   (b) Urial
(c) Arabian Oryx   (d) Wild Goat

437. It is a taboo to pass under this tree during the night. Which is it?
(a) The Devil Tree   (b) Pilu
(c) Peepal   (d) Tamarind

438. 'Prosperity is measured by the number of....

stacks'. Which word completes this once popular western belief?

(a) Chimney   (b) Firewood
(c) Hay   (d) Smoking

439. Which plant is religiously installed before the doors of a Hindu house to ensure happiness?

(a) Coconut Palm (b) Indian Lotus
(c) Hibiscus   (d) Basil

440. The Inca civilisation measures the passage of time on the basis of the life cycle of a crop. Which is it?

(a) Potato   (b) Barley
(c) Maize   (d) Wheat

441. Which antelope is considered Lord Krishna's favourite and as a result has been extensively depicted in Indian paintings and sculptures?

(a) Tibetan Antelope
(b) Chowsingha
(c) Black Buck
(d) None

442. Which tree's fruit is offered to Hindu Gods and Goddesses instead of a human head?

(a) Kadamba   (b) Banana
(c) Coconut Palm (d) Wood Apple

Literature

443. Who wrote 'Water, water everywhere, not any drop to drink', which is now fast becoming a reality?
    - (a) T.S. Eliot
    - (b) Robert Browning
    - (c) W.B.Yeats
    - (d) S.T. Coleridge

444. What is considered a life-giving and life-supporting system in Vedic literature?
    - (a) Rain
    - (b) Cloud
    - (c) Stream
    - (d) River

445. Which famous novel describes the massive dust storms that occur in the USA, especially in the region known as the Dust Bowl?
    - (a) *Jungle*
    - (b) *The Grapes of Wrath*
    - (c) *The Pioneers*
    - (d) *The Last of the Mohicans*

446. Which tree is described by Kalidasa in *Ritusamhara*?
    - (a) Teak
    - (b) Banyan
    - (c) Ashoka
    - (d) Shami

447. 'Tiger, tiger burning bright/ In the forests of the night'. Who wrote these lines?
    - (a) William Blake
    - (b) Robert Frost

(c) William Wordsworth

(d) P.B. Shelly

448. Which wildlife region of India has been immortalised by Rudyard Kipling's jungle tales?

(a) Ranthambhor   (b) Periyar

(c) Kanha   (d) Palamau

449. Which nineteenth century classic correctly described the age-old practice of using man's wastes for increasing the fertility of farmlands?

(a) *The Hunchback of Notre Dame*

(b) *War and Peace*

(c) *Les Miserables*

(d) *The Mayor of Casterbridge*

450. Which wildlife region of India has been immortalised by Jim Corbett's hunting tales of man-eating tigers?

(a) Kumaon Himalaya

(b) Garhwal Himalaya

(c) Terai Himalaya

(d) All

451. Which poet said, 'Thou canst not stir a flower without troubling a star'?

(a) William Wordsworth

(b) W.B. Yeats

(c) P.B. Shelley

(d) Francis Thompson

452. Which famous Indian writer has written a Science Fiction short story on the destruction of the Silent Valley by a hydel scheme much before it came into the news?
    (a) Pottekat   (b) R.K. Narayan
    (c) Raja Rao   (d) O.V. Vijayan

453. Who wrote, 'Nature, it seems, is the popular name for milliards and milliards and milliards of particles playing their infinite game of billiards and billiards and billiards'?
    (a). Walt Whitman   (b) N.H. Auden
    (c) P.B. Shelley   (d) Piet Hein

454. Which eminent literary figure has written the novel *The Dean's December* describing the social effects of lead poisoning?
    (a) Kurt Vonnegut (b) John Updike
    (c) Salman Rushdie (d) Saul Bellow

455. Which play of the Norwegian playwright Henrik Ibsen staged in 1882 discussed environmental issues even contemporary today?
    (a) *An Enemy of the Public*
    (b) *Ghosts*
    (c) *A Doll's House*
    (d) All

XIII

INDIAN SCENE

General

456. Where is the Black-necked crane seen in India?
    (a) Arunachal Pradesh
    (b) Kashmir
    (c) Garhwal Himalayas
    (d) Ladakh

457. Where did the first recorded incident of release of hazardous waste occur in India?
    (a) Bhopal, MP
    (b) Thane, Maharashtra
    (c) Monghyr, Bihar
    (d) Kanpur, Uttar Pradesh

458. What percentage of land in India is under forest cover?
    (a) About 14 per cent
    (b) About 26 per cent
    (c) About 21 percent
    (d) About 18 per cent

459. The Mussoorie hills of the Doon valley are

being destroyed by this. What is it?

(a) Denudation   (b) Quarries

(c) Agriculture   (d) Mining

460. Which bird is on the verge of extinction in India in recent times?

(a) Eagle   (b) Vulture

(c) Flamingc   (d) Parrot

461. Which G.M. (Genetically Modified) crop recently came into news when it was cultivated illegally in India?

(a) Rice   (b) Cotton

(c) Wheat   (d) Jute

462. How long is India's coastline?

(a) About 7,000 km

(b) About 2,000 km

(c) About 10,000 km

(d) About15,000 km

463. Whose disposal is nowadays a growing cause of concern in India?

(a) Sewage waste

(b) Medical waste

(c) Agriculture waste

(c) Flyash waste

464. Which material is commonly used all over India to build houses?

(a) Mud
(b) Burnt bricks
(c) Reinforced concrete
(d) Cement blocks

465. Which source of water is nowadays being tapped on a large scale all over India?
(a) Fog   (b) Rain
(c) Snow   (d) Hail

466. Which aquatic animal has been released on a large scale in the Ganga to rid it of waste flesh?
(a) Gharial   (b) Turtle
(c) Dolphin   (d) Fishes

467. What fraction of land in India is lying waste as a result of environmental problems?
(a) One-fourth   (b) One-tenth
(c) One-third   (d) One-twentieth

468. Where is the National Museum of Natural History located?
(a) Mumbai   (b) New Delhi
(c) Kolkata   (d) Chennai

469. Why is the Silent Valley so called?
(a) It is silent during the night.
(b) It is silent during the day.
(c) It has nothing to do with silence.

(d) It is derived from its original Sanskrit name.

470. Which Indian river serves the largest cultivable area?
(a) Godavari   (b) Krishna
(c) Ganga   (d) Saryu

471. Which body has produced a state-wise forest cover map for India?
(a) Institute of Economic Growth
(b) National Remote Sensing Agency
(c) Forest Research Institute
(d) Space Applications Centre

472. Which Indian state has named all its tourist resorts after birds?
(a) Assam
(b) Kerala
(c) Andhra Pradesh
(d) Haryana

History

473. Emperor Akbar used this animal for hunting in the wild. Which one?
(a) Cheetah   (b) Wild dog
(c) Lion   (d) Leopard

474. Which Indian King or Emperor was fond of

watching birds and animals and of growing new plants and trees?

(a) Bahadur Shah (b) Thirumala
(c) Rama Raya (d) Jahangir

475. Which ancient Indian scientist claimed that termite mounds were indicators of groundwater?

(a) Khana (b) Garga
(c) Varahamihira (d) Solihotra

476. Which Indian King passed a law forbidding the felling of fruit-bearing trees for building ships because it adversely affected the peasantry?

(a) Sawai Jai Singh II
(b) Prithviraj Chauhan
(c) Surajmal
(d) Shivaji

477. Which ancient Indian text contains rules and regulations on how to run a protected forest, 'Abhayarnya'?

(a) *Chandogya Upanishad*
(b) *Arthasastra*
(c) *Mahasiddhanta*
(d) *Brahmasphuta-siddhanta*

Policy

478. When was the use of DDT banned for agricultural purposes in India?
    (a) 1962   (b) 1985
    (c) 1974   (d) 1951

479. Which forest area in India was first brought under control and protection?
    (a) Malabar   (b) Konkan
    (c) Garhwal   (d) Sunderbans

480. Which is the only Indian state that recognises the rights of people displaced by irrigation, power and other utility projects to get land in the area benefited by the projects?
    (a) Rajasthan   (b) Tamil Nadu
    (c) Maharashtra   (d) Gujarat

481. When was the first National Forest Policy formulated?
    (a) 1948   (b) 1980
    (c) 1964   (d) 1952

Acts

482. When did the Water (Prevention and Control of Pollution) Act come into operation in India?
    (a) 1969   (b) 1972
    (c) 1974   (d) 1976

483. When was the Air Pollution Control Act promulgated in India?
    (a) 1980   (b) 1981
    (c) 1982   (d) 1983

484. When did the Wildlife (Protection) Act come into operation in India?
    (a) 1965   (b) 1972
    (c) 1974   (d) 1982

485. When was the Environment Protection Act enforced in the country?
    (a) 1980   (b) 1986
    (c) 1982   (d) 1988

486. When was the Forest Conservation Act passed in India?
    (a) 1960   (b) 1970
    (c) 1980   (d) 1950

Energy

487. What do the Indian biogas plants need?
    (a) Firewood
    (b) Cattle dung
    (c) Agriculture waste
    (d) Kerosene

488. What is the major source of fuel in rural India?
    (a) Kerosene
    (b) Agriculture waste
    (c) Fuel wood and charcoal
    (d) Cow dung cake

489. Where was the first micro-hydel electric plant set up in India?
    (a) Nainital   (b) Mandi
    (c) Darjeeling   (d) Shimla

490. Which Indian state is the largest supplier of firewood to cities?
    (a) Madhya Pradesh
    (b) Uttaranchal
    (c) Andhra Pradesh
    (d) Bihar

491. Where is the sole Regional Wind Energy Test Station for adapting, evaluating and testing windmills built in the country located?

(a) Ahmedabad (b) Allahabad
(c) Bangalore (d) Jorhat

Dates

492. When was the Department of Non-conventional Energy Sources established?
(a) 1975 (b) 1980
(c) 1988 (d) 1982

493. When was the Department of Environment set up?
(a) 1975 (b) 1970
(c) 1962 (d) 1980

494. When was Project Tiger launched?
(a) 1960 (b) 1973
(c) 1967 (d) 1970

495. When was the Bombay Natural History Society founded?
(a) 1881 (b) 1883
(c) 1885 (d) 1887

496. When was the Central Ganga Authority constituted to guide and oversee the programme to restore the environmental balance of the river Ganga?
(a) 1980 (b) 1982
(b) 1985 (d) 1988

Disasters

497. Which of the following areas is highly prone to avalanches?
     (a) Manali   (b) Almora
     (c) Pir Panjal   (d) Dibrugarh

498. Which phenomenon has not yet affected the Indian coastal region?
     (a) Cyclone   (b) Tsunamis
     (c) Both   (d) None of the above

499. Which natural hazard does not occur in India?
     (a) Earthquake   (b) Flood
     (c) Volcano   (d) Landslide

XIV

QUOTES & RECORDS

Quotes

500. Who said, 'A forest is a perfect example of the law of return in action'?
    (a) Chandiprasad Bhatt
    (b) Richard St. Barbie Baker
    (c) Konrad Lorenz
    (d) H.Y. Mohan Ram

501. Who quipped, 'Brush your teeth with the best tooth paste, then rinse your mouth with industrial waste'?
    (a) Woody Allen (b) George Wald
    (c) Tom Lehrer (d) Barbara Ward

502. Who said, 'Pollution is nothing but the resources we are not harvesting. We allow them to disperse because we've been ignorant of their value'?
    (a) Konard Lorenz
    (b) Lewis Mumford
    (c) Claude Alvares
    (d) R. Buckminster Fuller

503. Who said, 'Serious pollutants do not respect national boundaries'?
   (a) Aldo Leopold   (b) Rachel Carson
   (c) John Kemeny   (d) James E. Carroll

504. Who said, 'It is time to choose between quantity and quality, between accumulating and sharing, between pleasure and joy'?
   (a) Gerald Durrell
   (b) F. Kenneth Hare
   (c) Jacques-Yves Cousteau
   (d) T.H. Huxley

505. Who said, 'You do not have to be an ornithologist, oceanographer, or biochemist to understand that the world around us is being abused'?
   (a) Jacques-Yves Cousteau
   (b) Salim Ali
   (c) Peter Borelli
   (d) Lewis Mumford

506. Who said, 'Chernobyl has once more demonstrated, as did Three Mile Island, that a nuclear accident any where is a nuclear accident everywhere'?
   (a) Alvin M. Weinberg
   (b) Robert Gale
   (c) Al Gore
   (d) Alvin Toffler

507. Who said, 'Acid rain was the first of a series of environmental dilemmas that have challenged traditional notion of national security and even state sovereignty'?
(a) Barry Commoner
(b) John E. Carroll
(c) Aldo Leopold
(d) Al Gore

508. Who said, 'The answer to the degradation of the environment lies not in less science but in more science'?
(a) Alvin Toffler   (b) H.K.Jain
(c) Rachel Carson   (d) Rene Dubos

509. Who said, 'Science gives us knowledge of our environment. It sets the scene in which we act'?
(a) Margaret Mead
(b) Magnus Pyke
(c) Herbert Spencer
(d) Jacob Bronowski

510. Who said, 'Conservation is still in the horse and buggy state while extinctions are happening at the speed of an Exocet missile'?
(a) Rachel Carson   (b) Gerald Durrell
(c) Anil Agarwal   (d) Al Gore

511. Who said, 'Ecologists believe that a bird in the bush is worth two in the hand'?
    (a) George Wald
    (b) Chandiprasad Bhatt
    (c) Stanley G. Pearson
    (d) Madhav Gadgil

512. Who said, 'Green politics today is the rediscovery of old wisdom made relevant in a different age'?
    (a) Jonathan Porritt
    (b) Rachel Carson
    (c) Margaret Mead
    (d) E.O.Wilson

513. Who said, 'The rainforests are being destroyed not out of ignorance or stupidity but largely because of poverty and greed'?
    (a) Michael H. Robinson
    (b) Kenneth E. Boulding
    (c) Barbara Ward
    (d) George Wald

Records

514. Which is the longest insect?
    (a) Silverfish   (b) Stick insect
    (c) Dragonfly   (d) Cicada

515. Which is the largest fruit?
- (a) Jackfruit
- (b) Pineapple
- (c) Watermelon
- (d) Papaya

516. Which is the world's oldest tree?
- (a) Bristlecone Pine
- (b) Douglas Fir
- (c) Mediterranean Cypress
- (d) Giant Redwood

517. Which is the largest continent?
- (a) Australia
- (b) North America
- (c) Eurasia
- (d) South Africa

518. Which is the fastest growing plant?
- (a) Cactus
- (b) Bamboo
- (c) Palm
- (d) Sandalwood

519. Which is the largest carnivore on land?
- (a) Malayan Sunbear
- (b) Indian Tiger
- (c) Siberian Tiger
- (d) Kodiak Bear

520. Which is the largest sea?
- (a) Arabian sea
- (b) South China sea
- (c) Red sea
- (d) Dead sea

521. Where are the largest tortoises found?

(a) Galapagos Islands
(b) Sri Lanka
(c) Island of Aldabran
(d) All

522. Where is the largest forest in the world located?

(a) Russia   (b) Scandinavia
(c) Argentina   (d) China

XV

MISCELLANY

523. When this spacecraft was launched, a nuclear disaster was feared. Which is it?
   (a) *Luna-8*   (b) *Galileo*
   (c) *Pioneer-11*   (d) *Viking-1*

524. In recent years, some countries have begun to feel the necessity of an international law concerning this. What is it?
   (a) Seas   (b) Ocean
   (c) Atmosphere   (d) Soil

525. Which is the latest form of pollution unleashed by science?
   (a) Genetic   (b) Electromagnetic
   (c) Magnetic   (d) All

526. Where is the campaign 'No Driving Today' taking place to fight smog?
   (a) New York   (b) Moscow
   (c) Bonn   (d) New Mexico

527. If fusion reactors are built in the future, the release of this chemical could be the major hazard. Which one?

(a) Deuterium   (b) Iodine
(c) Strontium   (d) Tritium

528. If the greenhouse effect becomes real and melts polar ice, which one of the following regions will first disappear under water?
   (a) Hawaii Island
   (b) Maldives
   (c) Island of Kiribati
   (d) Mauritius

529. Which day is celebrated as the 'World Environment Day'?
   (a) 2 February   (b) 19 July
   (c) 5 June   (d) 28 August

530. What is 'Environment Impact Assessment'.
   (a) Not an exact science
   (b) An exact science
   (c) A subjective science
   (d) An objective science

531. What led to the early thinking or awareness about environment?
   (a) Shrinking water sources
   (b) Shrinking lands
   (c) Declining human values
   (d) Rising epidemics

532. What is the real limit to development or growth today?

(a) Environmentally unsafe natural resources.

(b) Threat to resources not affecting world trade directly.

(c) Wasting of resources of all kinds.

(d) The capacity of the environment to deal with waste in all its forms.

533. To save forests and environment of the countryside all over the world, who should be educated?

(a) Men   (b) Women

(c) Children   (d) Politicians

534. Who founded the Club of Rome, an international body to formulate policies for the survival of mankind?

(a) Aurelio Peccei (b) Norman Myers

(c) David Baldock (d) Linus Pauling

535. What does CITES, an international law, deal with?

(a) Genetic resources

(b) Urban pollution

(c) Urban population

(d) Endangered species

536. Which series of satellites has surveyed cities, countryside and forests?

(a) *TIROS-N*   (b) *NIMBUS*

(c) *LANDSAT*   (d) *ATS*

537. Mud houses provided excellent insulation against this. What is it?
   (a) Heat   (b) Cold
   (c) Noise   (d) All

538. Which is considered to be the 'Golden Age of Environmentalism'?
   (a) Vedic Age   (b) Bronze Age
   (c) Stone Age   (d) None ever existed

XVI

PHOTO QUIZ

539. This insect-like spacecraft was used to study the earth and its environment, among other things. What is it? When was it launched?

540. Which is this lake? Where is it located? What is special about it?

541. This looks like the flare of an erupting volcano, but it is not. It is a cloud. What kind of cloud is it? What does it indicate about weather?

542. This is a common sight of an industrial plant. What is the purpose of the cylindrical tower in such a plant?

543. Yes, it is a deadly monster, but in a miniature form. What is it? What harm does it cause?

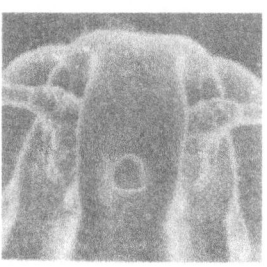

544. Is it a Maruti? No, it isn't! Then what is so special about this vehicle? Does it look different in any manner from the present-day vehicles?

545. What are those sharp pointed lines? What has produced them? What is their source?

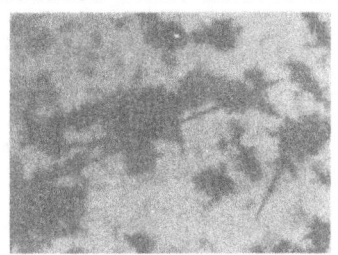

546. Identify this bird. If it is not possible to identify the bird, tell the reason why.

547. This is a special type of ship. What is so special about its deck?

548. An artist's conception of a future energy farm. What will it be called?

549. What is so special about these large barges floating near London? What are they doing?

550. Again, a special type of house built in France.
It is made up of novel material. What is it?

ANSWERS

1. (c)   2. (a)
3. (d) The near extinct animal is called 'Pere David's deer'.
4. (b)   5. (a)   6. (c)   7. (d)
8. (c)   9. (c)   10. (a)   11. (c)
12. (c)   13. (c)   14. (d)   15. (d)
16. (b) Hutton had forwarded the same idea but not scientifically compelling enough.
17. (b)   18. (d)   19. (d)   20. (b)
21. (d)   22. (b)   23. (b)   24. (c)
25. (b)   26. (c)   27. (c)   28. (a)
29. (d)   30. (d)   31. (b)   32. (d)
33. (b)   34. (b)   35. (d)   36. (d)
37. (b)
38. (d)Popular as 'Chico Mendes'.
39. (b)*Presbytis geei*. 40. (d)
41. (b)   42. (a)   43. (d)   44. (b)
45. (b)   46. (a)   47. (c)   48. (c)
49. (c)   50. (d)   51. (b)   52. (a)
53. (d)   54. (d)   55. (a)
56. (d) A resident of Death Valley in Nevada desert, U.S.A.
57. (b)   58. (d)   59. (d)   60. (b)
61. (c)
62.(a)Also known as 'Venezuelan oil bird'.

63. (c)   64. (b)   65. (b)   66. (d)
67. (b)   68. (c)
69. (b) Some forms, not all.
70. (c)   71. (c)   72. (b)   73. (c)
74. (d)   75. (c)   76. (c)   77. (c)
78. (b)   79. (a)   80. (c)   81. (d)
82. (c)   83. (b)   84. (d)
85. (d) The African elephant.
86. (c)   87. (b)   88. (c)   89. (b)
90. (c)   91. (c)   92. (b)   93. (a)
94. (b)   95. (c)   96. (c)   97. (c)
98. (d)   99. (d)   100. (c)   101. (c)
102. (a)   103. (b)   104. (b)   105. (a)
106. (d)   107. (a)   108. (c)   109. (b)
110. (d)   111. (d)   112. (d)
113. (c) Called 'Sweet track' after its discoverer,
     Raymond Sweet.
114. (a)   115. (d)   116. (a) and (b)
117. (a)   118. (b)
119. (d) At Catal Huyuk.
120. (b) Dharavi in central Mumbai.
121. (a)   122. (b) About 2000 B.C.
123. (b) Now in Persia.
124. (a) Leading to dumping of old technologies
     into the environment.
125. (d)   126. (d)
127. (a) Common space and facilities make it so.
128. (a)   129. (a)   130.(a) and (d)

131. (b)
132. (d) Two world wars forced people to flee their homes in Europe and other continents.
133. (a)   134. (c) Adopted in 1951.
135. (a)   136. (b) 137. (c)   138. (d)
139. (c)   140. (b) 141. (a)   142. (b)
143. (b)   144. (c) 145. (a)   146. (c)
147. (a)   148. (b) 149. (c)   150. (c)
151. (d)   152. (d) 153. (c)   154. (a)
155. (b)   156. (a)
157. (c) Success not clear.
158. (b)   159. (a) 160. (b)   161. (b)
162. (b)   163. (d) 164. (b)   165. (d)
166. (a)   167. (c) 168. (b)
169. (d) Sonic boom has been found to do superficial damage to badly built structures.
170. (c)   171. (b) 172. (b)   173. (a)
174. (d)
175. (b) About 27 per cent of the total household consumption.
176. (c)   177. (d) 178. (a)   179. (b)
180. (b) Ink contains lead.
181. (a) Releases fluorocarbons.
182. (a)   183. (b) and (c)   184. (a)
185. (c)   186. (b) 187. (a)
188. (b)   189. (b) A radioactive gas.
190. (d) Added to water as a disinfectant.
191. (d)   192. (c) 193. (b)   194. (a)

195. (a)   196. (b) 197. (d)   198. (c)
199. (a)
200. (b) and (c) 201. (c) 202.   (b)
203. (a)   204. (d) 205. (c)   206. (b)
207. (c)   208. (a) and (b)   209. (b)
210. (c)   211. (a) 212. (b)   213. (c)
214. (a)   215. (a) 216. (c)   217. (b)
218. (d) Half-life of 24,400 years.
219. (d)   220. (d) 221. (a)
222. (a) and (c) 223. (a)   224. (a)
225. (d)
226. (b) Called coal worker's pneumoconiosis.
227. (a)   228. (b) 229. (d)
230. (b) and (d) 231. (c)   232. (c)
233. (b)   234. (b) 235. (d)   236. (d)
237. (b)   238. (d)
239. (c) Felling of trees forces ticks to fasten on
     to labourers instead of their original hosts
     living on them.
240. (b)   241. (b) 242. (b)
243. (b) Due to proliferation of snails that
     harboured a deadly disease.
244. (a) and (b) 245. (d)   246. (a)
247. (a)   248. (a) 249. (d)   250. (d)
251. (a) and (b) 252. (a)
253. (d) Through rain water enters ground wa-
     ter.
254. Rachel Carson who wrote *Silent Spring*.

255. Shirley McGreal, who has set up the International Primate Protection League which fights for the rights of primates all over the world.

256. John James Audobon, an ornithologist par excellence.

257. George Adamson, who raised lions and released as many as 20 into the wild in Kenya.

258. Madhav Gadgil. 259. M.C.Mehta.

260. Romulus Whittaker. 261.(c)

262. (d)263.(b) 264.(d)   265. (b)

266. (b) Neritic, Euphotic, Abyssal, Benthic and Pelagic.

267. (a) According to the widely accepted theory.

268. (a)   269. (a) 270. (d)   271. (b)

272. (c)   273. (a)

274. (a) Water moves clockwise in spring and summer and anti-clockwise in autumn.

275. (d)   276. (b) 277. (a)   278. (b)

279. (d)   280. (d) 281. (c)

282. (a) Passage of earth through their remnants.

283. (c)   284. (b) Laika.   285. (a)

286. (c)

287. (a) Remnants of spacecraft, rockets and satellites.

288. (b)   289. (d) 290. (a)   291. (c)

292. (c)   293. (b) 294. (a)   295. (a)

296. (d)   297. (d) 298. (b)   299. (d)

300. (c)   301. (a)   302. (d)   303. (d)
304. (a)   305. (a)
306. (b) Surface, soil and crown fires.
307. (b) and (c)   308. (a)   309. (d)
310. (d) Scholars differ on this issue.
311. (c)   312. (c)   313. (d)   314. (b)
315. (c)   316. (a)   317. (b)   318. (b)
319. (b)   320. (b)   321. (b)   322. (d)
323. (b)   324. (a)   325. (d)   326. (b)
327. (a)   328. (b)
329. (d) Appiko means 'Chipko' only – to hug the tree.
330. (d)   331. (d)   332. (c)   333. (c)
334. (d)   335. (b)   336. (b)   337. (b)
338. (d)   339. (d)   340. (b)
341. (c) Thanks to David Wingate.
342. (d)   343. (d)   344. (c)   345. (c)
346. (a)   347. (d)   348. (a)   349. (b)
350. (c)   351. (d)   352. (b)   353. (c)
354. (d)   355. (a)   356. (a)   357. (a)
358. (a)   359. (b)   360. (b)   361. (b)
362. (a)   363. (a)   364. (a)   365. (b)
366. (b)   367. (d)   368. (a)   369. (a)
370. (a)   371. (b)   372. (d)   373. (a)
374. (b)   375. (b)   376. (a) and (b)
377. (b)   378. (b)   379. (d)   380. (a)
381. (d)   382. (b)   383. (c)   384. (a)
385. (b)   386. (c)   387. (c)   388. (a)

389. (b)   390. (d) 391. (b)   392. (c)
393. (a)   394. (b) Geneva Protocol.
395. (c)   396. (a) 397. (c)   398. (b)
399. (d)   400. (a) 401. (b)   402. (b)
403. (d)   404. (a) 405. (b)   406. (b)
407. (b)   408. (c) 409. (c)   410. (b)
411. (a)   412. (b)
413.(d) 21 countries which agreed to reduce sulphur dioxide emissions by 30 % form the club.
414. (b)   415. (c)   416. (b)   417. (a)
418. (c)   419. (a)   420. (c)   421. (b)
422. (a)   423. (a)   424. (d)   425. (c)
426. (b)   427. (c)   428. (b)   429. (b)
430. (b)   431. (d) 432. (c) Space Age.
433. (a) *Bhumi puja.* 434. (d)   435. (d)
436. (c) By eating its meat; Arabs believe its noble qualities of bravery, strength and endurance can be absorbed.
437. (c) and (d)   438. (d)
439. (d) *Tulsi.*   440.(c)   441. (c)
442. (c)   443. (d) 444. (d)
445. (b) John Steinbeck is the author.
446. (c)   447. (a)448.(c)
449. (c) Victor Hugo is the author.
450. (a)   451. (d) 452. (a)   453. (d)
454. (d)   455. (a) 456. (d)
457. (c) In 1968, the Ganga river was set aflame

from the discharge of oil from a refinery effluent.

458. (a)
459. (b) The hills are rich in limestone.
460. (b)   461. (b) 462. (a)   463. (b)
464. (a)   465. (b) 466. (b)   467. (c)
468. (b)   469. (a) 470. (c)   471. (b)
472. (d)   473. (a) 474. (d)   475. (c)
476. (d)
477. (b) Kautilya is its author.
478. (b)
479. (a) In 1803, the East India Company declared Malabar forest a reserve forest as it contained teakwood needed for building ships.
480.(c)   481. (d) 482. (c)   483. (c)
484. (b)   485. (b)
486. (c) An amendment of Indian Forest Act, 1927.
487. (b)   488. (c) 489. (c)
490. (a) The former M.P.
491. (b) More stations are likely to be installed soon.
492. (d)   493. (d) 494. (b)   495. (b)
496. (c)   497. (c) 498. (b)   499. (c)
500. (b)   501. (c) 502. (d)   503. (d)
504. (c)   505. (c) 506. (a)   507. (b)
508. (b)   509. (b) 510. (b)   511. (c)

512.(a)   513. (a)

514. (b) The longest found in Indonesia measure more than 30 cm.

515. (a)   516. (a) 517. (c)   518. (b)

519. (d)   520. (b) 521. (a) and (c)

522. (a) and (b)

523. (b) Plutonium powered the spacecraft.

524. (c)

525. (a) Release of genetically engineered organisms.

526. (d)   527. (d) 528. (c)   529. (c)

530. (a)   531. (b) 532. (b) and (d)

533. (b) Women handle the energy and food requirements of a family and are also in constant touch with the next generation.

534. (a)

535. (d) Convention on International Trade in Endangered Species.

536. (c)   537. (d) 538. (d)

539. The U.S. spacecraft Skylab launched in 1973, which returned to the earth in 1979 as a space debris.

540. Lake Baikal in Siberia; it contains one-fifth of the world's total fresh surface water.

541. Cumulonimubus, a typical thunderstorm cloud which yields heavy rain, snow or hail.

542. Cooling tower of a plant meant to cool hot gases produced inside before releasing them

into the atmosphere.

543. Head of a locust under an electron microscope; it can devastate a green field in no time when it gathers in swarms.

544. An electric car; it runs on batteries and produces no emissions or smoke.

545. Tracks of cosmic rays coming from the outer space.

546. A seabird drenched in an oil spill.

547. It contains a sea water-desalination plant aboard its deck.

548. A solar energy farm.

549. The barges contain tightly sealed household waste which is being transported to a landfill.

550. The house is made of grass!

SCORE YOURSELF !

Count the correct answers you have given and mark yourself as follows:

Average: if 450–474 answers are correct.

Good: if 475–499 answers are correct.

Excellent: if 500–524 answers are correct.

If you score more than 525, you are a **SUPER GENIUS** in environment.